'You'd better go, Kirk.' It was very hard to speak the words when her treacherous body yearned for him to stay. But Jessica had known many years ago that Kirk could never be for her, and she knew it again now.

'Jessica . . .'

'Go. Now!'

He looked down at her, and she was certain that he meant to kiss her again. But he stopped away from her. A moment later he had closed the door behind him.

Another book you will enjoy
by ROSEMARY CARTER

ECHOES IN THE NIGHT

Believing that her half-brother Todd had been unfairly treated by Jason Langley's Adventure Tours company, Nicola determined to put the record straight. She joined the expedition to the Drakensberg as camp cook, and soon discovered that Jason was not what she had expected at all . . .

CERTAIN OF
NOTHING

BY
ROSEMARY CARTER

MILLS & BOON LIMITED
ETON HOUSE   18-24 PARADISE ROAD
RICHMOND   SURREY   TW9 1SR

First published in Great Britain 1991
by Mills & Boon Limited

© Rosemary Carter 1991

Australian copyright 1991
Philippine copyright 1992
This edition 1992

ISBN 0 263 77435 X

Set in Times Roman 10 on 11¼ pt.
01-9202-54240 C

Made and printed in Great Britain

CHAPTER ONE

'LAURA, I'm here!'

'Mommy?' The little girl had woken out of a nightmare. Her body shook with sobs and her face was wet with tears.

'No, honey... I'm Aunt Jess.'

Through her tears, Laura peered up at the face of her mother's identical twin sister. 'Mommy,' she insisted, and clung to her aunt.

Jessica put her arms around the child and held her close. With one hand she stroked Laura's hair. It was soft and smooth and very fair, very much like Jessica's and Linda's hair had been at the same age. Her eyes were the same vivid shade of green too. Laura was still shuddering, though not quite as violently as before. She was only four years old—far too young, Jessica thought through her own grief, for a little girl to lose both her parents.

'Mommy——' Laura said again.

'Stupid! That's not Mom,' said an angry voice. 'She's just Aunt Jess. Mom and Dad died in the accident. Don't you know that yet, Laura?'

Jessica looked across the room at her nephew. Framed in the doorway, he was a small, angry, defiant figure. She could see him quite clearly, for the nightlight had been left on in the room. Donny's hair, as dark as his sister's was fair, was tousled. Tufts of it seemed to stand permanently on end; not even for the funeral had Jessica been able to tame it. His fists were tightly clenched. Donny was not quite six.

'Come here, Donny,' Jessica said softly.

5

'Why should I?'

'You could sit on my lap with Laura, and we could talk for a while.'

'Nothing to talk about,' he said flatly. 'Anyway, I only sit on Mom's lap. And she's dead.'

'I know, honey. And I'm awfully sad, just as you are. But sometimes it helps to talk about things.'

'Don't need help. Not like Laura—she's just a baby. You'd think she'd know you weren't Mom.'

'She does know, Donny.'

Jessica's heart went out to her nephew. Though he did not know it, she was more worried about him than she was about his sister, who could give expression to her grief even while she tried to deny the reason for it.

Donny had not cried at the funeral. To Jessica's knowledge, Donny had not cried at all since the moment, a few days earlier, when the children had learned of their parents' boating accident in the choppy waters of False Bay off the shore of Cape Town. There was so much hurt in the child, but he would not allow himself to break down and give rein to his feelings. Jessica longed desperately to pull him into her arms and hold him close. Maybe then he would cry.

But she knew better than to force him into an intimacy he did not want. He would only push her away and withdraw even deeper into himself.

'Laura's stupid,' he said fiercely.

Kirk... As if from nowhere, a face came into Jessica's mind. She stared at the little boy in surprise. Donny so resembled his father, Tom, that Jessica would smile whenever she saw them together. Yet at this moment, flushed, angry and rebellious, he reminded her not of Tom, but of his arrogant older brother.

She shook her head, as if to erase an unpleasant memory, and held out a hand to the child. 'Maybe you'd both like some hot chocolate?'

'OK...' Donny's voice was choked suddenly. His shoulders drooped and his lips quivered slightly.

Kirk was gone. Donny resembled his father once more.

The children went to the kitchen with Jessica. Donny knew where the chocolate was kept, and Laura fetched a saucepan from the cupboard. Huddled in their fleecy pyjamas, they watched as their aunt warmed milk on the stove, then stirred in the chocolate.

Carrying a tray with three steaming mugs and a dish of biscuits, Jessica led them back to Laura's room. Laura crawled beneath the sheets, while Donny curled up in a big wicker armchair. Jessica sat on the edge of Laura's bed and watched the children sip their chocolate.

She began to talk to them as they drank. Deliberately, she steered away from the reality which each child seemed to be handling in its own way. Instead, she told them stories of long ago. Stories about two little girls, Linda and Jessica, who had been so alike that almost nobody, sometimes not even their parents, could tell them apart. What pranks they had played, and what good times the twins had had together. And then she told them a funny story about a young boy called Tom; it was a story which she had once heard from Linda.

Gradually the eyelids of the children took on a heavy look. As Jessica took the empty mugs from their hands she decided it did not matter if their teeth were not brushed this once.

'Sleep well,' she said softly as she bent and kissed them in turn. Laura put her arms around Jessica's neck and held her tightly a few seconds. Even Donny did not balk at his aunt's embrace. He let her hold him a moment before he went back to his own room.

When the children were asleep, Jessica tiptoed out of the room. The chocolate had left a too-sweet taste on her tongue, and she went to the kitchen, where the percolator was still plugged in. She poured herself a mug of coffee and took it to her bedroom. Too restless to get into bed, she went to the window and looked outside.

To the young woman whose home was in a busy area of Johannesburg, the night silence of the Cape winelands was strangely intense. Beyond the window, and stretching all the way to the mountains, lay the vineyards of Bergview. The last harvest had been a wonderful one, Linda had written, just a month ago. Tom was so looking forward to the wines those grapes would make. But Tom would not see the wine now.

The harvest was not the only thing Linda had talked of in her letter. Jessica took it from the top drawer of her dresser again now. It was beginning to look tearstained and ragged, for she had read it so often that she could have recited the important parts from memory.

...if anything should ever happen to Tom and me— not that it's likely—I want you to look after my darling children for me. Will you, Jess, please? I suppose I should talk to Tom about having some kind of official document drawn up, but, in the meantime, you do promise you'd care for them, don't you?

Other than you and Mom and Dad, there's only Kirk, and can you honestly remember a time when it was easy to get in touch with Mom and Dad? As for Kirk, that man doesn't know a thing about children. Besides which, if he were to get married—and I think he might, to a perfectly awful woman called Alicia Mason—he wouldn't have much time for Donny and Laura anyway.

Kirk... Six and a half years ago at Linda's wedding, Jessica had thought him the most handsome, the most exciting person she had ever met. Not half an hour in his company, and she had been sure she was in love with him. Only when his hostility towards Linda had become apparent had Jessica recognised his arrogance. But

Tom's and Linda's wedding had taken place despite Kirk's angry opposition, and Jessica had not seen him since then. It was a long time, she told herself now, since she had given so much as a thought to his existence.

She looked once more at the letter, and into the silence she said, 'You have my promise, Linda.'

She went to bed then. Only now, in the darkness of the unfamiliar room, could she let the fullness of her grief overcome her. All day she had tried to keep her sadness at bay, for she had known she had to be strong for the children. Finally she was free to weep.

The stories Jessica had told Donny and Laura were only a small part of the life she and Linda had shared. Two little girls, born within five minutes of each other twenty-four years ago, they had shared a closeness which only other twins could fully appreciate. Their mother had often told them they had had their own language as babies; a language of sounds and gestures which nobody but they themselves could understand. Until Linda's marriage, they had not needed many friends. They had almost never quarrelled, had never been apart a day.

Their parents were archaeologists, always away on a dig in some far-flung corner of the world, and while the twins were young they had all travelled together. Later, when they went to school, the little girls had lived with their grandparents for many months at a time, while their parents unearthed the secrets of ancient civilisations in areas of the world that were so remote that often they did not even have access to a telephone. They were in Italy now, but temporarily away from their base, so that Jessica had not even been able to reach them in order to let them know about the accident.

Perhaps because they were so dependent on each other for comfort and company, Jessica and Linda had developed a special intuitiveness which only a few twins possessed. When Linda had been punched by a bully,

Jessica's face had ached. When Jessica had tumbled off a high cliff at a school picnic and lay unconscious in a lonely stretch of veld, Linda knew where to find her.

On a bright Sunday morning in Johannesburg, just a few days ago, Jessica had suddenly known—even before the phone call that summoned her—that hundreds of miles away in Cape Town something terrible had happened.

'I'm taking the children home with me,' Jessica said the next day.

'To *Johannesburg*?' The housekeeper, who had been at Bergview since Tom was a baby, looked askance.

'I work there, Betty. I have to get back.'

Betty shook her head. 'They don't know that place.'

'I have a little house and a garden. Nothing anywhere as grand as Bergview, of course, but I'll get a swing and a sandpit so that the children can play. I'll find a nice nursery school for Laura, and a school for Donny, and in the evenings, when I get home from work, they'll be with me.'

'Johannesburg is not their home, Miss Jess.'

'I know that, Betty. It isn't ideal, but Laura and Donny will be fine, once they get used to the change. Really they will. Oh, I know they'll miss this wonderful place, and they'll miss you even more, but they'll be with someone who loves them very much.'

'Mr Kirk, he won't like it.'

'I don't think Kirk will mind,' said Jessica. 'It's not as if he's used to small children. If anything, I should think he'd be greatly relieved that he doesn't have to be responsible for Donny and Laura.'

The housekeeper did not answer, but she looked unhappy.

After a moment, Jessica said, 'I know Kirk's in France—doing some kind of business in the wineries there, I suppose. How long do those trips of his usually last?'

'Three weeks, sometimes four. He's only been away two weeks, but he'll be back, Miss Jess, I know he will. Just as soon as he hears about the accident.'

'Maybe so, but I can't wait for him, Betty. I have a job in Johannesburg, and I have to get back.'

Later that morning, Jessica phoned the advertising agency where she worked as a commercial artist. Her employer, who had been a little put out when she'd left the office so abruptly, was relieved to know she would be back at her drawing-board by the beginning of the next week.

Laura had become Jessica's shadow, following her wherever she went. The moment Jessica sat down the little girl would climb on to her lap. Sometimes she cried and asked for her parents, but it seemed to Jessica that she was beginning to understand that they were not coming back.

Donny was as unreachable as ever. He refused to talk about the accident. Moodily he stalked about the house, resisting Jessica's every attempt to put her arms round him. She had seen him in the yard, hitting the oak tree with a stick, one savage stroke after another until his sticks broke. Sometimes she watched him hurl heavy stones across the ground, his face damp and red with the effort. Donny was angry and unhappy, and Jessica, her heart going out to him, wished she knew how she could comfort him.

She decided to start that very day to prepare for the move. Waiting until the children were playing together on the swings in the back yard—she did not want to upset them with her preparations—she went to Laura's room, where she began to make piles of clothes. The necessities as well as a few favourite toys would accompany them on the plane. Betty would parcel up the rest and send it by post.

For more than an hour Jessica sorted and folded and made notes on an ever-growing list, only stopping now and then to look out of the window to watch the children at play. Donny's dark head shook or nodded emphatically when he spoke; Laura's fair hair was like early wheat in the sun. It warmed her heart to see what good friends they were.

She was folding a faded sweater of Laura's when she heard the door open. Betty, she thought, and turned with a smile. A smile that faded as she stared, shocked, at the man who stood in the doorway.

In his ashen face, her own shock was echoed. '*You...*' he whispered.

'I'm Jessica,' she said quickly, realising his mistake.

'Yes, of course.' Already, just seconds later, Kirk was beginning to recover his composure. 'Just for a moment I thought you were... Stupid of me. I'd forgotten how alike you and Linda were.'

'Hardly anyone could tell us apart,' she said unsteadily.

His gaze was on her face. 'I thought *I* could. I remember something in the eyes that was different... I'm very sorry,' he said then. 'I know how close you were to Linda.'

'I'm sorry too, about Tom.' Her voice shook.

'Yes, I know.'

'When did you get back, Kirk?'

'A few minutes ago. Our lawyers managed to contact me. As soon as I heard the news I got on to the first available plane.'

'I suppose you know the whole story, then?'

'Some of it, though not all. You'll be able to fill me in on the rest later. Where is everybody? The children? Betty?'

Save for a few new lines around his eyes, his appearance was as Jessica remembered it, long, lean body exuding an animal sinuousness which was as disturbing now as it had been all those years ago. He was a superbly built man, tall, narrow-hipped and broad-shouldered, with hair as dark as Donny's and grey eyes that were deep-set and intelligent.

'Betty's in the kitchen,' she said. 'Donny and Laura are playing in the back yard. I'll call them, I know they'll want to see you.'

She was moving towards the open window when she was stopped by a hand on her arm. At the touch of his fingers on her bare skin, she tensed.

'Wait a moment,' he said. 'I want to know what you're doing here.'

He was a little too close to her, intruding upon her space in a way that made her far too aware of him. She took a step away from him, and saw the glitter in his eyes as he dropped his hand.

'I came for the funeral.'

'Not that. I mean here—in Laura's room.'

'I'm sorting things.'

'The suitcases…' He gestured. 'I get the feeling you're packing.'

Until this minute Jessica had felt at ease at Bergview. Suddenly she was uncertain.

'I'm taking Donny and Laura back home with me. I won't be able to take all their clothes and toys on the plane with me, so Betty will——'

'With whose permission?'

'*Permission?* I don't need anyone's permission to care for my niece and nephew!'

'You need mine,' he said flatly.

So the old arrogance was still there.

Jessica made herself meet his eyes coolly and without any sign of self-doubt. 'I can't imagine why I'd need that.'

'I'm the children's guardian.'

'No, Kirk, I am.'

'Really? When did that happen?'

'Linda wrote me a letter. She asked me to look after Donny and Laura if anything were ever to happen to her and Tom.'

'I find that hard to believe.'

'She wanted a promise from me.'

Kirk's eyes flicked her face. 'This letter—was it a legal document? Signed by them both? Witnessed?'

I suppose I should talk to Tom about having some kind of official document drawn up... Jessica felt a flicker of fear as she remembered the words.

'That wouldn't have been necessary. Not between Linda and me,' she said, with a firmness she was far from feeling.

'That's where you're wrong. You'll have to face it, Jessica—I'm the children's guardian. I have been since they were born. They go nowhere unless I say so.'

Jessica went pale. 'Linda wanted her children to be with me. She didn't want you to look after them—she said so.'

'If that's the way she felt—and I have only your word for it—then evidently she didn't make her wishes clear.'

'But she did. I have the letter—it's in my room. I can show it to you.'

'I'm not disputing the fact that Linda may have written to you, but I am the guardian according to the will, Jessica. It's the only document that has any value. Surely you must understand that?'

She looked at Kirk, and felt a little ill. He seemed so certain of his facts, this big, attractive man who was so unlike his brother. Come to think of it, Kirk was unlike any man she'd ever known. Which was not something she could let herself think about at this moment.

'Where is this will?' she demanded. 'I'll have to see it.'

'With our lawyers in Cape Town. It's too late to go there today, but I'll make an appointment for tomorrow.'

'I think you'd better.'

'In the meanwhile, I suggest you empty out that suitcase and put Laura's clothes back in the cupboard.'

Jessica looked down at the sweater in her hands. Linda had knitted it. It was pink, with a border of little white rabbits. Jessica remembered how Linda, never an expert knitter, had battled with the intricacies of the pattern.

'Forget the rabbits,' Jessica had advised, laughing. 'The sweater will be just as pretty without the border.'

'Laura picked it out,' Linda had said.

'She won't know the difference.'

'It's what she wants, Jess, and I hate to disappoint her. I'm not giving up lightly—not yet.'

Jessica could not give up lightly either.

She looked up at Kirk. 'I will not abandon my sister's children. If you are in fact the legal guardian, I suppose I'd have to defer to you before making important decisions. But that doesn't mean Donny and Laura have to live here with you. Linda asked me to look after them, and I will.'

She was totally unprepared for the hands that gripped her shoulders, pulling her towards him.

'I forbid you to take my brother's children away from this estate!'

'Forbid? That's strong language, Kirk.'

'Do you understand?'

Through the thin fabric of her blouse, she could feel every one of his fingers. Her heart began a painful thudding.

'Let go of me!' she said through tight lips.

'Do you understand?'

She shook her head. 'You don't know what you're asking of me.'

His hands tightened, and she felt herself being drawn even closer against him. Their bodies were not actually touching, and yet they might as well have been, for despite the few inches of space between them she could sense the hardness of his limbs and the heat of his skin. He was holding her just as he had held her six and a half years ago at Linda's wedding. There was the same anger in him now as there had been then. Also the same aura of danger and sexuality.

In that moment Jessica knew why she had waited until now to return to Bergview; why she had found it necessary to shut Kirk Lemayne out of her mind.

'I'm waiting for an answer,' he said.

Jessica forced herself to still her trembling as she looked up into a face that was all hard lines and sensuous lips and gaunt cheekbones.

'I can only give you my answer when we've been to the lawyer,' she said.

Abruptly, Kirk dropped his hands. 'I'm going outside to see Donald and Laura.'

'I'll come with you.'

'I know my way, Jessica.'

'If there's a chance—even an outside chance...that what you say is right, I want to see how the children relate to you.'

Kirk's eyebrows lifted at that, but he made no comment when she walked out of the room with him.

To get to the back yard they had to walk through the kitchen, where Betty was rolling pastry on the big wooden table. At the sound of their footsteps she turned, and her face lit in a great smile of relief.

'Mr Kirk! You're back!'

'Are you all right, Betty?'

'It's been very bad, Mr Kirk.'

'I know. I wish I'd been here, but I came as soon as I heard the news.' He went to her and put his arm around her shoulder. 'You can stop worrying now. I'll take care of things from here on.'

'I know that,' she said, and, as Kirk moved on towards the door, Jessica saw a hint of tears in the housekeeper's eyes.

In the yard, the children were still playing on the red double swing. Absorbed in their game, they did not see their aunt and uncle coming towards them. Jessica thought Kirk would call out to them, but he did not. Instead, he stood quite still about ten feet away from the swing. Curiously, Jessica glanced up at him. In his eyes was an unexpected gentleness. There was something else too—an expression of unutterable sadness.

He must have felt her looking at him, for his head turned, and for a long moment their eyes held. Jessica had the strangest feeling that each knew exactly what the other was thinking. And then Kirk took a step forward and the moment was broken.

'Laura... Donald!' he called as he approached the swing.

Laura was the first to look up. 'Uncle Kirk!' she shouted as she jumped off the swing and ran along the grass into his arms.

'How's my sweetheart?' For a moment Kirk held the child close to him. Then he looked across at the little boy, who had not moved off the swing. 'Hello, Donald.'

To Jessica, who had never heard her nephew addressed as anything but Donny, the name had a strange sound.

She looked at the silent child. He sat on the red seat, staring at his uncle, his expression closed and unreadable.

'I've come all the way from France, Don. Aren't you going to say hello to me?'

Donny looked away. He did not answer.

Kirk watched him a moment longer. Then, still holding Laura, he advanced on the swing, scooped the little boy from his seat, and swept him up into his arms as well.

Jessica held her breath as she watched Donny. He had made himself quite rigid, so that for a moment she wondered how Kirk was going to be able to hold both children. Suddenly the stiffness went out of him. Jessica heard a stifled gasp, then Donny had collapsed against Kirk, his head huddled against the broad chest.

'There now, Don, boy, there now.' Kirk spoke very softly. 'Everything's going to be OK.'

The child did not answer, but Jessica saw that he was shuddering. With his face out of sight in his uncle's rough sweater, Donny was finally able to weep.

Betty brought a pitcher of lemonade and four tall fluted glasses outside to the veranda. There was also a dish of warm scones just out of the oven.

'Cheese scones—my favourites!' Kirk smiled at Betty. 'You must have known I was on my way home.'

'I told Miss Jess you'd come.' As if she knew that Kirk would solve whatever problems there might be, the housekeeper looked happier than she had done since the funeral.

Betty went back into the house, and Jessica poured the lemonade. When the children had finished their drinks, Kirk pulled two tiny yellow spinning tops from the pocket of his trousers.

'Hey, look what I brought for you,' he said, and sent one of the tops spinning along the glass surface of the table.

Moments later the children were trying out the tops themselves, a little distance away on the smooth black stone floor of the veranda. Donny was able to spin his top right away. For Laura it was more of a problem; the little yellow top flopped over every time she tried to send it flying.

'Donald has a knack for it,' said Kirk, who was watching them play.

'Laura will get it right too in time. Kirk, I notice that when you talk to Donny you call him Donald or Don.'

'That's right, I do.'

'He's always been called Donny.'

'Not by me, he hasn't. I've called him Donald from the day he was born, and I'm not about to start calling him Donny now.'

'Why not?'

The rugged face turned her way. 'Donny... You seriously want me to call my nephew Donny? Think about it, Jessica—what do you think that name does for his self-image?'

'*His self-image?* Donny's not quite six years old. Calling him by an affectionate name can't harm him.'

'Wrong, Jessica. Call him Donny, and there's a danger that as he grows up he'll think of himself as something less than a man.'

'That's ridiculous!'

The gaze of the dark-haired man skimmed her face, lingering on her stormy eyes and flushed cheeks. He had an inherent sexuality that made her nerve-ends feel raw.

'I want so much for Tom's son. I always did,' Kirk said. 'I want him to face life with courage. I want him to be honest and tough and independent.'

'You want him to be just like you,' Jessica said slowly, almost without thinking.

'You made the comparison; I didn't,' he said.

He grinned at her suddenly, the expression in his eyes one of pure devilment. Jessica could only hold that gaze a few seconds. Then she had to look away.

CHAPTER TWO

JESSICA stepped out of the shower and into her bedroom. She had washed her hair; there was just enough time for it to dry before dinner. She had lovely hair, fair and shining, with a soft natural wave which looked nicest when she left it to dry on its own, and so long that it reached way down beneath her shoulders.

On her bed lay one of her favourite casual outfits—mauve and pink patterned skirt and a matching mauve blouse with an ornamental front zip that ran from the waist to the high mandarin collar. On the floor were open-toed sandals, white with a strip of mauve leather around the edges.

Jessica slipped on the skirt, then the blouse. She was pulling up the zip when her fingers met with resistance. As she bent her head to see the problem, she felt as if someone was pulling hard at her scalp. A thick strand of hair was caught in the zip.

Grimacing at the pain which came when she moved her head even slightly, Jessica tried to pull the zip down, and when that did not work she tried pulling it upwards. With no success. If anything, her hair became only more tightly entangled.

What now? She opened the door of her room and called into the passage, 'Betty...?'

No answer from the housekeeper.

'Betty?' she called again. 'Laura or Donny? Please, I need some help!'

Still no answer from anyone. And then the door of the room next to hers opened and Kirk emerged.

'Something wrong, Jessica?'

20

'I was looking for Betty.'

'Why?'

'It doesn't matter why. Won't you just find her for me?' said Jessica, thinking that if Betty did not come soon there would be nothing for it but to find a pair of scissors with which to cut through the thick wet strand of hair. That done, she would be able to work more easily at loosening the remaining hair from the zip.

Kirk's eyes sparkled with amusement as he took in the situation in a moment. 'You appear to have a problem.'

'You could say that!'

'And it just so happens that I'm a whizz with zips.'

She looked at him, knowing he would think her childish if she insisted on calling the housekeeper when he could obviously help her.

'This is really the darnedest thing,' she said as he followed her into her room.

'It's also very sexy.'

Something in his tone made her look at him again. He was eyeing her in such a way that her pulses began a sudden racing.

Her gaze shifted from his. 'I'd do it myself, but I only seem to make things worse each time I try.'

'Do you know how you look, Jessica, with all that untidy wet hair? No make-up—that flush in your cheeks?'

'Find Betty—or get on with it yourself,' she ordered, as firmly as she was able.

'This isn't the Jessica I thought I knew—cool, on top of every situation. Jessica, who looks like Linda, yet isn't like Linda at all.'

Her throat felt dry suddenly. 'Why do you talk this way, Kirk? You hardly know me,' she said unsteadily.

'I know you intrigue me.'

He was getting to her, just as he had got to her six and a half years ago. And she would have to shut him out of her mind when she left Bergview, just as she'd had to do then.

'I think you'd better go,' she said.

'And leave you in this predicament?'

'I'll manage on my own.'

'Ah, but I want to help you.'

She made herself stand quite still as he stepped up close to her and began to work on the zip.

'Quite a tangle,' he said after a few seconds.

'That's why I needed help.'

'Am I hurting you?'

'No...'

In fact, he was more gentle than she would have imagined possible. A few tugs on her scalp were unavoidable, but she hardly felt them. She was far more aware of Kirk, the man, bending over her, too close to her; of breath that was cool on her flushed cheeks and forehead; of a sensuous mouth just inches from her own. Desire sprang to life inside her, a primitive yearning that was unlike anything she had experienced with any of the other men she had dated.

'There you are,' he said, just when she thought he would never finish.

'Thank you.' Her voice was jerky. 'I don't know what I'd have done without your help.'

'You'd have managed. I have a feeling you're a resourceful lady. Fact is, if you'd done it alone, I'd have been done out of a memorable experience.' He laughed softly.

He was still holding the zip, but one finger was on her throat now as well, moving slowly along the smooth skin, lingering on the spot where the telltale pulse beat far too quickly.

'You can go now,' she said unsteadily.

'When we've made sure this thing works.'

'It works.'

'I need to see that for myself.'

'Kirk!' she protested, and put a hand over his.

But he was too quick for her. With one movement he pulled the zipper all the way up to her neck. With the next, he'd tugged it down to her waist.

'*Bastard!*' she shouted, and lifted a hand to strike his face.

Again he anticipated her. He caught her hand in one of his, and held it. With his other he pushed apart the edges of her blouse. She saw his eyes on her throat and on the swell of her breasts above her bra. And then his fingers followed the trail his eyes had taken, lingering at the base of her throat, stroking the swell of her breasts and the hollow between them. The touch of his fingers on her bare skin was soft, deliberately soft, and all the more tantalising for it.

By the time his mouth covered hers, fire was scorching through her veins. His arms were around her, and she could feel the beating of his heart against her throat.

The kiss was not long, nor even terribly passionate. Yet for all that, it was for Jessica, who at the age of twenty-four was certainly not unkissed, the sweetest thing she had ever experienced.

When Kirk lifted his head she pulled away from him. She was shaking.

'Why did you do that?' she threw at him.

'I wanted to.'

'You'd better go, Kirk.' It was very hard to speak the words when her treacherous body yearned for him to stay. But she'd known many years ago that Kirk could never be for her, and she knew it again now.

'Jessica——'

'Go. Now!'

He looked down at her, and she was certain he meant to kiss her again. But he stepped away from her. A moment later he had closed the door behind him.

Jessica walked into the dining-room, hoping to find the children already at the table. But Kirk was there alone. He was standing at the sideboard, his back to her. Jessica was about to leave the room when he turned. There were two glasses in his hands.

'You look lovely in mauve,' he said, as he came towards her.

She saw him glance at the zip. How tempted she had been to change out of the wretched blouse, but she had decided against giving him the satisfaction. When he looked up again she saw the laughter in his eyes.

'Bergview wine,' he said, as he handed her a glass.

She did not take it from him. 'I don't think so, Kirk. It doesn't seem quite right to be drinking alcohol. It's such a short time since...'

The laughter went out of his face. 'Think of it as a tribute to Tom and Linda,' he said quietly. 'This was Tom's favourite wine. I made it from the grapes which he planted. Linda loved it too.'

And what had Linda's feelings been for the man who had made this wine? True, her twin had not wanted Kirk to care for her children. But had she ever compared him with his brother, and found Kirk stronger, more masculine, more attractive than Tommy? Infinitely sexier?

Appalled by the fact that she could even think such a thing, Jessica reached for the glass. Just for a moment, Kirk's fingers touched hers, and she knew he was thinking of their kiss.

She took a sip of the wine, which was every bit as good as its reputation. Then, needing to put some space between Kirk and herself, she stepped away from him and looked around her. The house, with its curving white Cape Dutch gables and its lovely spacious rooms, fascinated her. The dining-room, cool and gracious, was in keeping with the rest of the house. Jessica had not had a meal here before: alone with the children, she had preferred to eat in the alcove off the kitchen. But to-night, with Kirk back home, things were different. Betty had insisted that they eat here.

In the centre of the room stood a great stinkwood table. Around it were eight matching leather-seated chairs. The curtains were a dark amber velvet, the floor was made of yellow-wood, and on the walls hung pictures of Bergview as it must have looked a hundred years ago.

'I'd forgotten quite how gorgeous this house is,' Jessica said. 'All this incredible wood . . . It looks as if it's been here always.'

'In a way it has been. The table has been in this room since the day my great-grandparents came to Bergview as newlyweds.'

'I wish I could have seen it then,' she said. 'It's a little like living in a very beautiful museum, isn't it, Kirk?'

'Do you like the feeling?' His eyes were on hers, his expression enigmatic.

Jessica laughed. 'If you could see my little house in Johannesburg, you'd hardly need ask! It can't begin to compare with this—tiny rooms, view on to a busy street. Bergview is wonderful.'

'Interesting that you should feel that way. I don't think Linda shared your feelings for the place. In fact, I doubt that she was ever really happy here.'

'Of course she was happy!'

'Was she, Jessica? I thought sometimes that Linda would have much preferred a nice modern house in Cape Town, with big picture windows and edge-to-edge carpets and a view over the ocean.'

'You don't know that...' Jessica began, then stopped. For Kirk was right. Her sister had never been altogether at ease in this beautiful farmhouse with its massive furniture and antiques.

Just then the children made their appearance. Laura came into the room at a run. Donny walked more slowly, dragging his feet across the wooden floor.

When they had all sat down to supper, Laura drew Jessica's attention to the shirt she was wearing. It was pale blue, with a darker blue Eiffel Tower emblazoned across it.

'Look what Uncle Kirk brought from France, Aunty Jess.'

'It's very nice.' Jessica smiled at her. 'I see you've got one too, Donny.'

'Yeah...'

'Do you like it?'

'It's OK.'

Jessica glanced across the table at Kirk. His expression did not change as he met her eyes. It was as if he was telling her that Donny would emerge from his withdrawal when he was ready to.

Betty had gone out of her way to make a special meal in honour of Kirk's homecoming, but with Donny in this dismal mood the atmosphere was leaden. Jessica did her best to make bright conversation. Unfortunately, most of her openings led nowhere, for Donny refused to respond, while Laura, affected by her brother's deliberate silence, had grown quiet as well.

Now and then Jessica glanced at Kirk. He began to tell the children a funny story about his travels. Laura started to laugh, but Donny looked at her so contemptuously that after a moment her laughter faded. Kirk's eyes were on his nephew, and his expression was thoughtful.

They were still busy with their main course when Donny began to bang his spoon against his glass.

'Stop that, Donald,' ordered Kirk.

Donny eyed his uncle, and went on banging.

'I asked you to stop playing with the spoon, Donald.'

Kirk's voice was friendly but firm. And for a while Donny did, in fact, obey.

Now there was silence in the dining-room. Jessica searched her mind desperately for something to say. She had just thought of a funny anecdote about Linda and herself, when the banging began once more. Donny was kicking the table leg at the same time now. His face was openly rebellious, as if he was daring his uncle to take action. Laura, watching her brother, looked frightened.

'If you don't stop that immediately, you'll have no dessert, Donald,' Kirk said.

Betty had already told them that dessert was to be apple tart and ice-cream. The little boy looked so shocked at the idea of being deprived of such a treat that Jessica felt sorry for him. Kirk was wrong, she thought, to make such a big deal of something that did not matter very much. Especially now...

'Maybe, just this once, we could overlook this...' she began.

Kirk gave her an icy look. To Donny, he said, 'I meant what I said.'

The atmosphere around the table had become charged. Kirk had the look of a man who would not hesitate to give effect to his warning. There was a hint of moistness in Donny's eyes, but his expression had lost none of its rebelliousness. In that moment Jessica was reminded again of the likeness she'd noticed the first day between uncle and nephew.

She held her breath. Laura appeared equally tense. But nobody would ever know if Donny meant to continue his provocative behaviour, for at that moment the door opened and a woman walked into the room.

'Kirk!' she cried. '*Darling!* I just heard half an hour ago that you were back.'

She glanced around the table. As her eyes lit on Jessica, she seemed taken aback. And then she gave a thin smile. 'But of course, it's only Jessica, isn't it? I saw you at the funeral.'

'I'm sorry, I suppose I should know you, but there were so many people.' Jessica wondered how she could have possibly forgotten this dramatic-looking woman.

Her face was hard but beautiful. Jet-black hair and huge dark eyes, meticulous make-up. Skin that was tanned and smooth as marble. Tall and slender in figure-hugging trousers and jacket, she could have been a model.

'You two haven't been introduced?' Kirk said. 'Alicia, this is indeed Linda's sister, Jessica Bartlett. Jessica—a good friend of mine, Alicia Mason.'

So this then was the Alicia of Linda's letter. Actually, it was not the first time Linda had mentioned her. 'Cold as a fish and only interested in Alicia,' she had said once. 'She's out to get Kirk, and chances are she'll be successful. Not that I'd mind ordinarily—those two deserve each other—but life will be grim if that woman ends up living at Bergview.'

Alicia had gone to Kirk's chair. Standing behind him, she put her arms around his neck and leaned her cheek against his. 'How awful this terrible accident must have been for you, darling! Having to rush back so suddenly. I'm so sad about poor Tom.'

'It's been very bad,' Kirk agreed. 'Worst of all for Donald and Laura. But it's been bad for Jessica too. Linda was her twin.'

Jessica looked at Kirk, surprised yet pleased that he had spoken for her.

'Yes, of course—ghastly! Such a shock for all concerned.' Alicia glanced from the children to Jessica, and Jessica was appalled to see that there was only token sympathy in her expression.

Dropping her arms from Kirk's neck, she pulled out the chair next to his and sat down. 'I have so much to tell you, darling. You wouldn't believe the things that have happened while you were away. Did you hear what went on with the Mallors? No? And you'll never believe the news I have about Mitch De Villiers. Oh, you don't know how glad I am that you're back. It's never the same here when you're away, and——'

She stopped only when Betty came into the room carrying a tray with apple tart and ice-cream and one extra plate. There was coffee too. Alicia looked a little put out when Betty put the tray down in front of Jessica.

When Betty had left the room and Jessica had poured the coffee, Alicia said, 'Staying at Bergview long, Jessica?' Her voice was like ice.

'I can't really tell,' Jessica said, very politely. 'I've made no decisions yet.'

Involuntarily, she looked across the table at Kirk. His eyes gleamed and his lips were slightly tilted.

She looked away from him. Briskly she began to dish up dessert. Donny started on his, quickly, before his uncle could decide otherwise. Jessica only touched the food on her own plate.

The moment the children had finished eating, she said, 'If you'll excuse us ... I'll go and see Donny and Laura to bed.'

'I think they can manage on their own,' Kirk said.

'I want to tell them a story or two before they go to sleep.'

'Join us again afterwards.'

'Maybe I will,' Jessica said, but she knew full well that she would do nothing of the sort.

Jessica bathed Laura. Donny was too old to be bathed, and she only ran his water. When both children were in their pyjamas, she asked them to choose a book for her to read to them.

Laura was more interested in talking. 'Donny and me don't like Alicia,' she said. She could not say the name properly yet, so it sounded like Alyshia.

'She seems like a nice lady,' Jessica said mildly.

'She's going to marry Uncle Kirk.'

'You don't know that, stupid,' Donny said fiercely, with more emotion than he'd shown in days.

'Aunty Jess, can you marry Uncle Kirk?' Laura asked wistfully.

'No, honey, I can't.' Jessica picked up a book and turned the pages firmly. 'Now, then, are you ready to hear this story about the puppy that ran off into the woods?'

Leaving the children in Betty's care, Jessica and Kirk drove to see Bergview's lawyers the next morning. The road from the winelands to Cape Town was very beautiful, but although Jessica loved the scenic beauty of the Cape Peninsula today she had no eyes for it. It was impossible for her to appreciate the winding passes, or the spectacle of the vineyeards stretching towards the purple mountains, when her mind was on a document in a lawyer's office.

It was windy as they drove into Cape Town. Cloud swirled around the flat summit of Table Mountain, and the ocean was flecked with white. The offices of Smith and Walters were in a tall building in Adderley Street, the main thoroughfare of the city. Kirk introduced Jessica to Mr Smith, who shook both their hands and told them how sorry he and his partners had been to hear of the accident.

Jessica sat tensely through the formal pleasantries. Coffee was brought into the room, but after a token sip she pushed it aside. Her muscles were taut as she watched Mr Smith settle himself behind his leather-topped desk. Looking from one to the other, he reached for a file and opened it.

'You're here to talk about the will.' His manner was businesslike now.

'One particular aspect of it,' said Kirk.

Unable to endure the suspense a moment longer, Jessica leaned forward in her chair. 'Kirk says he's the children's guardian.'

'That is correct, Miss Bartlett.'

'But that can't be right, Mr Smith!'

'I have the will right here. Tom asked me to draw it up three years ago.'

'He did? Maybe Linda didn't know what was in it.'

'It was signed by them both, Miss Bartlett. Right here, in my office.'

From her bag, Jessica drew the letter. She gave it to Mr Smith.

'Those are my sister's latest wishes,' she said when he had read it. 'You can see by the date that it was written very recently.'

The lawyer looked across the desk at Jessica. Her cheeks were flushed and the fingers clutching her handbag were tight.

'I hope you'll believe me, Miss Bartlett, when I say that I understand how you feel.'

'But you're unwilling to do anything about it.'

'It's not a matter of being unwilling. I can only deal in fact and in law. I believe when your sister wrote you this letter she was perfectly sincere in her wishes——'

'Yes, she was! She made it very clear that she wanted me to take care of Donny and Laura if anything were ever to happen to her and Tom. And I feel certain those must have been Tommy's wishes too. They always wanted the same things for their children.'

'Then they should have taken steps to make their wishes legal. It would have been easy enough for me to draw a new document. A simple codicil to this will would have taken care of things.'

'That was Linda's intention. You can see that from the letter...'

'Perhaps it was her intention,' the lawyer said, quite gently. 'Perhaps it was what both of them wanted. We'll never know. The fact remains, at this point we have to go by the will.'

'No!'

'Yes,' Mr Smith said. He handed the document across the desk. 'Why don't you take a look at this, Miss Bartlett?'

Though Jessica had not once turned her head to look at Kirk, she was intensely aware of him in the chair next to her. He had remained silent throughout her interchange with the lawyer. Was he gloating now? With the will in her hands, she turned and looked at him—and was surprised to see a hint of sympathy in the eyes that met hers.

The lawyer had marked the relevant page of the document. It took Jessica less than half a minute to read the guardianship clause. She read it twice again, just to make sure there was nothing she had missed.

When she looked up again the flush had gone from her cheeks and her face was pale.

'Unfortunately, it's clear enough. Kirk is Donny's and Laura's guardian.' She looked from one watching man to the other. 'But even then... Isn't there *something* that would change things?'

'There is one thing,' the lawyer said slowly. 'If for some reason Kirk were unwilling to assume guardianship, he could have you appointed in his place.'

'That's it, then!' For the first time there was hope in Jessica's voice.

'There's something you don't seem to have heard, Jessica.' Kirk's tone was dry as he spoke for the first time. 'I would have to be an *unwilling* guardian.'

She turned in her chair and looked at him. Any sympathy was now gone. His mouth had never looked more unyielding, his eyes more firm.

'You mean to stand on your rights, Kirk?' she demanded.

'I mean to carry out my brother's wishes.'

'And Linda's wishes? What about those? This letter... written such a short time ago... It's as if Linda had a premonition that something was going to happen.'

The lawyer shifted in his seat, and Kirk said, 'Don't get carried away, Jessica.'

'But it is so! Linda wanted me to take care of her children.'

'I have to say it again. If that was what she wanted, then your sister should have had something drawn up to that effect,' the lawyer said. 'I understand how you feel, Miss Bartlett. But I'm afraid you have to face it— Kirk Lemayne is the legal guardian of Tom's and Linda's children.'

Jessica was so despondent after they had left the lawyers' offices that she failed to notice that Kirk had not taken the national road to Paarl and Stellenbosch and the winelands. It was a while before she realised that they were in Constantia, a lovely area with winding roads and flowering shrubs and ancient trees.

'This isn't the way back to Bergview, is it, Kirk?'

'I thought we'd have lunch before we go back.'

'I wish you'd asked me first. I'm really not in the mood to eat,' she protested.

'You won't improve the situation by not eating. Besides, I'm hoping you'll be tempted when you see where I'm taking you.'

'I have a lot of thinking to do, Kirk.'

'We both have. But the thinking will keep—it always does. It's been a long morning, Jessica. It will do us good to have some quiet time together before we drive any further.'

The lunch-hour had not yet begun, and the car park of the outdoor restaurant was still quite empty. Jessica stiffened as Kirk came round to her side of the car and took her arm, but he seemed not to notice that as he led her to the garden where a waiter gave them a choice of tables and left them with menus.

When they were alone, Kirk smiled at her. 'Now, then—see something you fancy?'

'I meant what I said. I'm not in the mood for lunch.'

'I am. And I think you would be too, if you'd only let yourself relax.'

The garden was peaceful and beautiful. There were flowers and shrubs everywhere: pink and white azaleas; a delicate jasmine; roses, velvety red and a little overblown; a protea with a few huge, spiky blooms. The air was heavy with perfume and alive with the incessant droning of bees.

'What will you have, Jessica?'

'You don't know how to take no for an answer,' she grumbled, only half meaning the protest at this point.

'Ungracious wench,' he said, but he was grinning at her. 'All right, then, if you haven't learned yet how to make up your mind, I'll have to order for both of us.'

He did—double helpings of anchovy toast, scones with fig jam and cream, a pot of coffee.

'Sound tempting?' he asked, when the waiter had gone.

'You know it does. I think there's a bit of the magician in you, Kirk.'

'Wonderful!' His grin had grown wider.

'Don't think I meant that as a compliment. Here we are in this lovely restaurant, about to eat scones and cream, just as if nothing had happened. But something *has* happened, Kirk. My sister is dead, and so is your brother.'

'Do you think I'm not as unhappy as you are?' In an instant his smile had vanished.

'You'd have to be unhappy about Tommy,' she said slowly.

'And about Linda. She'd become part of my family too.'

'Then can you tell me why we've come here?'

'Because for the children's sake, as well as our own, we have to keep going.'

'The children . . . I kept hoping you were wrong about the will. Have you any idea how upset I am at the way things have turned out?'

'Of course. That's partly why I brought you here. You need time to calm yourself before we go back.'

'Don't presume to know what I need, Kirk. I'll tell you what I need. I need to find a way of keeping the promise I made to my sister. I know exactly how I feel about what happened today. And I'm not likely to feel any differently tonight or tomorrow or next month.'

His eyes were on her face. 'And you're determined to talk about it right now.'

'Yes, I am. I know you'd prefer to treat this meal as an interlude. But that would mean making small talk, and I don't think I can cope with that at the moment.'

'All right, then,' he said. 'Why don't you say what's on your mind?'

Jessica looked at Kirk, and saw the seriousness in the gold-flecked eyes. He was listening. And she wished things were otherwise, that she could be carefree and flirtatious with him. She had never met a man who could compare with him. Nobody with whom she felt so alive, so challenged, so utterly feminine.

But there it was, Kirk was Tom's brother, and because an outdated document had never been re-drawn, he had become her adversary.

'How can I persuade you to relinquish your guardianship?' she asked abruptly.

'You can't.'

'Why not? It won't always be easy for you to have the children around.'

'I could say the same for you, Jessica.'

'I'd make a plan,' she said impatiently. 'I'd find a way of handling any situation.'

'Precisely what I'll do too,' said Kirk. 'I think you should remember that Donald and Laura are Lemaynes.'

'For what it's worth.'

'It's worth more than you might think. You already know that Bergview has been in our family for more than a century—five generations, to be exact. It's Donald's and Laura's heritage. One day the estate will be theirs; they'll share it with any children I might have.'

Kirk's children. With Alicia? If only the idea did not hurt so much.

'I understand,' Jessica said quietly. 'And yet I can't face giving them up. I love those children, Kirk. I love them as much as if they were my own.'

'Maybe you do.' There was a strange expression in his eyes.

'You sound doubtful—as if you don't believe me.'

'I believe you, Jessica. But there's something I don't understand. In all the years since Tom and Linda were married you never once came to Bergview. If you really love the children as much as you claim to, surely you'd have made an effort to see them?'

'I did see them, whenever Linda and Tom came to Johannesburg. You don't know how much I used to look forward to their visits.'

'Which doesn't change the fact that you never once came to Bergview. Six and a half years, Jessica. That's a long time.'

'As a matter of fact,' she said, moving restlessly in her seat, 'I did come.'

'Really?' His eyes narrowed. They lingered on her face in a way that unnerved her.

'Quite a few times, actually.'

'Never when I was there.'

'Maybe not...' She was beginning to feel rattled.

'Why was that, Jessica?'

'Is this an interrogation?'

'I'm just curious.'

'Heavens, Kirk...' she tried to speak flippantly, 'how do I know why you were never there? Coincidence, I suppose. You always seemed to be away on one trip or another.'

'Or maybe,' he said softly, 'it was simply that you wanted it that way.'

CHAPTER THREE

'I DON'T believe this conversation!' Jessica's throat was dry suddenly.

Kirk's eyes never left her face. 'I believe you knew exactly when I'd be away, and that you planned your visits accordingly every time.'

'Why on earth would I do that?'

'Could it be that you were scared of me?' he drawled.

'Scared?'

She was angry now, for he was getting too close to the truth. Green eyes sparked fire as she glared at him.

'I was right in my assessment of you the first time we met. You really are an impossibly arrogant man, Kirk! You flatter yourself if you think I was ever scared of you.'

'Do I? Seems to me there has to be a reason why you went out of your way not to run into me again.'

Jessica shrugged. It was as much as she could trust herself to do.

'We were attracted to each other from the first moment we met, Jessica. Do you remember?'

'One meeting, Kirk, more than six years ago.'

'A meeting with sparks. You can't deny it.'

There had indeed been sparks. Jessica remembered the feeling of electricity, the way the air seemed charged with a special quality when she and Kirk were in the same room. Even Linda had noticed it. 'Careful, Jess,' she had warned. 'Kirk is ruthless. When he wants something, he lets nothing stand in his way. You don't want to fall for him.'

38

Jessica shifted her eyes from Kirk's. 'If there were sparks—and I'm not saying you're right—all they led to was an argument.'

An argument in which he had held her in such a way that she had been hoping he would kiss her.

'You said some terrible things, Kirk.'

'Did I?'

'You accused Linda of using pregnancy to trap Tom into marriage.'

'I remember.'

'What you said was unforgivable. I still feel the same way about it now as I did then. It takes two to make a baby, Kirk, I remember telling you that at the time. If there was any fault, then your brother was as much to blame as my sister. They both knew what they were doing when they made love.'

'Tom thought Linda was protected.'

'Did it ever occur to you that it was up to them both to be responsible? Besides, accidents happen.'

'And sometimes they're not accidents at all.'

'Why don't you say quite plainly what you mean?'

'Linda was young and insecure. Her parents were always away at some dig or other, and her sister—you, Jessica—had her thoughts on an education. Did you ever think that maybe Linda saw Tom and Bergview as a haven?'

'No, I did not! But even if it did happen that way— and I don't believe for a moment that it did—it wouldn't account for your rage. Linda and Tommy loved each other. Sooner or later they would have got together anyway. What was so wrong about their marriage?'

'They were both far too young. Linda was seventeen, Tom had just turned nineteen. He planned to go to university—he was going to study agriculture. It's what I did. Instead, he was saddled with a wife and a baby long before he was ready for them.'

'It would have been better if they'd both been older, I agree. But as for pregnancy being a trap—I'm really shocked to find out that after all these years you still believe Linda planned the pregnancy deliberately.'

'She wouldn't have been the first woman in history to do that.'

His eyes were like steel suddenly. It was a look which would come back to haunt Jessica, just as she would remember his tone when he spoke.

'It's the oldest story there is, Jessica. I've always despised any woman who would stoop so low as to fall pregnant on purpose.'

'You really are the very worst kind of chauvinist!' Jessica's hands were tightly clenched on the table top and her lovely green eyes were stormy. 'You want to know why I never came to Bergview when I knew you'd be around, Kirk? How could I, when I knew we'd end up at each other's throats?'

'There's no reason why that should happen this time.' His eyes had a wicked sparkle as he grinned at her. He looked so intensely attractive that her anger intensified. She did not want to let herself be affected by Kirk Lemayne.

'The fact is that it happens every time,' she said.

'It doesn't have to be that way. I hadn't even thought of the argument until you dredged it up. Six and a half years is a long time, Jessica. Why don't we just put the whole thing behind us?'

Unexpectedly he reached for one of her hands. It was still tightly clenched, but Kirk did not let that deter him. Folding his big hand over her small one, he stroked her fingers gently, persuasively, until at last they seemed to have no choice but to relax. He proceeded to thread his fingers through hers then; they were warm and hard and kindled fires in her veins, and Jessica discovered that she did not have the will-power to resist him.

'Better. Much better,' he said, his smile a mixture of mischief and devilment.

The waiter was approaching with their order, and Jessica took the moment to disentangle her fingers from Kirk's. It did not matter to her that the waiter must think they were lovers. What mattered was that she was beginning to wish more and more that it was true.

She poured the coffee and handed Kirk a cup. She added milk to her coffee, but Kirk preferred to drink his black. The anchovy toast was crisp and tangy, and the scones, which they decided to leave for last, looked delicious. A lone bee settled on the rim of the jam-jar, but Kirk waved it calmly away.

Two more couples had arrived, but the garden tables were spaced in such a way that people did not disturb one another. The sound of conversation was an indistinguishable hum that blended with the hum of the insects.

Kirk began to talk of other things. He wanted to know what books Jessica liked reading, what type of music she enjoyed, and whether she was as good a tennis-player as Linda had been. And Jessica rose to his questions, even though she knew that the conversation was a deliberate diversion. With the tension of the old argument out of the way, it was so extraordinarily pleasant to sit in the sunny garden with this most attractive of men that despite herself she began to relax.

It was only when they were in the car once more and driving back to Bergview that she said, 'There's something I don't understand. Since you felt so strongly about Linda's pregnancy—the baby that was Donny—I'd have thought you'd be only too happy to have me take the children off your hands.'

His eyes left the road for a moment as he turned to look at her. 'I don't feel that way at all.'

'You must see Donny and Laura as an obligation. They're Lemaynes, so you think it's your duty to force them to live with you at Bergview.'

'Duty doesn't come into it,' he said deliberately. 'I love the children. It doesn't matter how I felt all those years ago—that's history now. I love Donald very much. I love both children.'

'You'll be much too strict with them. Especially with Donny.'

'You're thinking about last night.'

'If Alicia hadn't arrived...if Donny had gone on banging the spoon...would you really have forbidden him to have dessert?'

'Yes.'

'He's a baby, Kirk. And just think what he's been through.'

'He's not a baby, Jessica. He knew exactly what he was doing.'

'Maybe...But he's lonely and unhappy and insecure. He misses his parents.'

'Agreed. That's why he's looking for attention—we both know that. But Donald has to understand that we love him even when he isn't being disruptive.'

'I don't like to see him punished, Kirk—especially now.'

'Do you think I enjoy it, Jessica? Is that really what you think?' His voice was flat.

'I don't know what to think.'

'I'm not an ogre. I'm a man who's just lost a brother and a sister-in-law, and who feels desperately sad for their children. It isn't easy for me to be strict with Donald, Jessica. That's something you don't seem to understand.'

'No, I don't. I happen to believe there's a time to be strict, and a time to overlook things and let them go. Maybe we have different views about raising children.'

'Maybe we do.'

'The children need me, Kirk. I hate to leave them.'

'Then don't.'

'I beg your pardon?' she said, after a startled moment.

Once more he turned his eyes from the road. 'You could stay at Bergview.'

Jessica was as unprepared for the suggestion as she was for the sensation of pure pleasure that shot through her at Kirk's words. 'That's obviously impossible,' she said then, wishing he didn't attract her so intensely.

'If you say so,' he drawled.

The moment they arrived at Bergview Jessica threw down her jacket and her bag and went to the phone. Her employer was glad to hear from her. Stewart Evans, an up-and-coming man in the advertising world, was thirty, divorced, and had made clear his interest in Jessica. He was jovial until he heard that she wanted another week of leave. Then he was firm.

'It's been too long already, Jess. The work's piling up, I need you back.'

'Just one more week, Stewart.'

'You said you'd be back on Monday.'

'Yes, I know, but I need more time. Stewart, please!'

'Three extra days, Jess, and that's it. I don't mean to sound unfeeling—I know what you've been through—but the work has to be done.'

Jessica decided to wait until the day before her departure to tell the children she was leaving Bergview. They were having supper, the four of them seated around the big stinkwood table.

'Don't go, Aunty Jess,' Laura pleaded.

'I have to, honey. I have to get back home.'

Laura jumped off her chair, climbed into Jessica's lap and flung her arms round her neck. 'Please, don't go!' she begged.

Jessica looked across the table at Kirk, but if she had hoped for any help from him it was not forthcoming:

his expression was impassive. She looked at Donny, who was rolling breadcrumbs on the tablecloth. His eyes were down and he refused to look at her.

Jessica addressed both children. 'Uncle Kirk will be here, and Betty too. They'll take good care of you.'

The arms around her neck tightened.

'I'll visit you often,' she said, and felt tears gathering in her eyes.

'Who cares anyway?' said Donny. 'You're such a stupid baby, Laura.' With that, he got off his chair, pushed it roughly out of his way, and ran from the room.

Jessica looked at Kirk. His eyes glittered, but he said nothing.

It was warm and lovely on Jessica's last day at Bergview, and Kirk suggested they have a *braaivleis* in the garden instead of eating indoors. Betty defrosted a few steaks and a length of *boerewors*, and made her special jellied vegetable salad which had always been loved by all. Dessert was a surprise, she said.

'What is it, Betty? Please, Betty, what is it?' begged Laura.

At last Betty gave in. 'Chocolate mousse with marshmallows,' she said, and was rewarded by happy looks from both children.

Kirk took charge of the meat, turning it now and then with a long-handled fork. He opened a small bottle of Bergview wine and he and Jessica had a glass each while they waited for the meat to cook. Laura and Donny played with a ball nearby. If the next day's leavetaking was on all their minds, nobody mentioned it, and Jessica was glad of it. She wanted this night to be untroubled and special.

Untroubled it was until the moment, midway through the meal, when Donny got up from his chair and began to swing a cricket bat dangerously close to the table.

'Move away if you're going to do that, Donald,' said his uncle.

Donny came closer still to the table. Round and round went the bat. Jessica held her breath as a bottle was almost knocked to the ground.

'Donny!' she protested.

At the sound of her voice he stopped. Very briefly he looked at her, and in that second she saw there were tears in his eyes.

And then the bat began to swing once more.

A pattern, Jessica thought uneasily. It was all too much like the first night. Only then Alicia had walked in before anything could happen. What could stop the inevitable now?

'Stop that, Donald,' said Kirk, very calmly.

Donny went on swinging.

'Move away, Donald, or something will break,' Kirk said.

The words had barely left his lips when there was a loud crash. A glass jug fell off the table, shattering glass all over the ground.

There was an awful moment of silence. Donny's arm froze in mid-air, and for a few seconds he looked like a small stone statue. And then Laura started to cry.

'It was an accident,' Jessica said quickly, before Kirk could speak. She felt as distraught as Laura.

'No,' said Kirk, 'it was no accident. Why didn't you listen to me, Donald?' His voice was as calm as before, but Jessica heard the steel in it.

'Broken glass means good luck,' she said, as reassuringly as she could. 'I'll get a brush and pan, and I'll sweep it all up in no time.'

'Why did you go on doing that when I told you not to?' Kirk asked the child.

'Because.'

'Go to your room.'

'You can't make me.' Donny's voice was high.

'Donald!'

Jessica, who saw the lovely evening disintegrating, put a hand on Kirk's arm. Beneath her fingers she felt the hardness of taut muscles.

'Not tonight,' she said very softly, so that only Kirk could hear the words. 'Please, not tonight.'

Abruptly he moved his arm away from her hand. 'Now, Donald,' he said.

For a few seconds it seemed as if the little boy would defy him. He stood his ground, his eyes wild, his mouth working as he looked from his aunt to his uncle.

'I hate you!' he cried suddenly. 'I hate you, I hate you, I hate you!' And then he ran into the house.

'Did you have to do it?' Jessica was furious as she confronted Kirk an hour later.

Both children were asleep at last. Jessica had just come from Laura's room, where matted lashes showed her that the little girl had been crying. She had checked on Donny as well, but he was huddled beneath the blanket, invisible but for a few strands of dark hair on his pillow, so that it was impossible to guess the state he was in.

'What other choice did I have?' Kirk's rugged face was bleak.

'You could have ignored it—treated it as an accident.'

'We both know it wasn't an accident. Just as it wouldn't have been an accident the other day if something had broken.'

'My last night here, Kirk, and you chose to spoil it.'

'Donald spoiled it when he knocked down the jug,' Kirk said quietly.

'That's ridiculous! Donny is five years old.'

'Almost six. Look, Jessica, we've been over this before. I feel as badly about what happened as you do, but you know very well that we couldn't overlook it.'

'You could have made light of it. You could have *pretended* it was an accident, even if you knew better. I don't believe Donny meant the jug to break.'

'I don't believe it either. I think he was as shocked as anyone by what happened.'

'Aren't you contradicting yourself, Kirk?'

'No, Jessica, I'm not. Donald was playing for attention. He'd been asked to stop swinging the bat, I warned him something would break, yet he went on.'

'I still think it could have been handled differently.'

'You'd have patted him on the head, and said, "Don't worry, honey, we can always get another jug."'

'Something like that.' She lifted her chin at him. 'All right, Kirk, I understand you're mocking me, but that's exactly what I would have done.'

'And you'd have taken one more step towards turning your nephew into a brat.'

'Wrong! I'd have saved an evening that was very precious to me. *My last evening at Bergview.* I have no idea when I'll be able to get leave from work again, when I'll get to see the children. And you had to ruin it.'

'It's your choice to see it that way.'

'It's the only way I *can* see it. Are you going to come down hard on Donny for every misdemeanour, Kirk? Are you going to make him a frightened, insecure boy?'

'That's what he is now, Jessica—frightened and insecure, and terribly unhappy because of it. I meant what I said the other day when I told you I love Donald. I want to see him become confident and independent. That way he'll be happy, and you and I will be proud of him.'

Jessica looked up at the tall dark-haired man. 'We both want the same things for the children,' she said.

'I think we do.'

'It's our ideas that differ—radically.'

He did not answer. He just stood there, looking down at her.

'The other day you said I had an option, Kirk. That I could stay at Bergview.'

'I still say it.'

His eyes were hooded, and so enigmatic as they lingered on her face that Jessica had to quell a sudden trembling.

'It wouldn't work.' She swallowed over the dryness in her throat. 'We'd be arguing all the time. There isn't a chance that it could work.'

'Then tomorrow is really goodbye?'

'Yes,' she said, 'it's goodbye.'

Six and a half years earlier Jessica had been aware of electricity in the air when she'd been with Kirk in this same room. She felt it again now as they stood there looking at each other. Her muscles were tight as desire sprang to life deep inside her. A small smile played on Kirk's lips. Every inch of him was an exciting blend of strength and sensuousness—the long lean body, the hard cheekbones, the curve of his lips, the eyes that could be so unnerving. He had never looked more attractive to Jessica than he did tonight, when she was on the verge of leaving his home.

She tried to move away as he reached for her, but he captured her head in both his hands, his thumbs going beneath her chin, his fingers sliding through her hair, and then he kissed her, very lightly. In seconds the desire that already existed inside her flared out of control. When he lifted his head to look down at her, she could only nod.

This time, as he drew her against him, his arms went around her and he held her close. He began to kiss her again, but now there was no lightness. It was a hard kiss, searching, demanding a response which she was unable to refuse him. He did not force anything on her. Rather she gave him what he asked, so that when his tongue probed her lips she opened her mouth to him willingly.

Sanity returned to Jessica only when Kirk tried to draw her down on to the carpet with him. At that moment she realised what was happening; that she had given him to understand it was what she wanted. Appalled, she twisted her head away from his and pushed at his chest with her hands.

'No, Kirk. No!'

His arms tightened a moment, as if he could not believe she was denying him now. Then, as her hands continued to push at him, he let her go.

'You're still sure you want to leave Bergview tomorrow?' he asked, when she had moved away from him.

'I have to,' she said numbly.

'After what just happened?'

'It didn't mean anything.' She tried to say it lightly.

'Didn't it?' His glance was infinitely disturbing.

'No.' Her breath skittered in her throat.

'Well then, since we can hardly have a repeat performance in front of the children tomorrow, consider it your goodbye kiss, Jessica.'

He looked down at her, his eyes hard and mocking. Then he turned and strode from the room.

Jessica dreaded saying goodbye to the children. After a night in which she had tossed and turned and barely slept, she did not even let herself dwell on the thought of saying goodbye to Kirk.

She took her farewell of Betty just before she left Bergview. The two women hugged, and Betty said, 'I'll take care of the children.'

'I know you will, Betty.'

'I hope you'll come back soon, Miss Jess.'

They all piled into the car then, Jessica in front with Kirk, Donny and Laura at the back. There was a point where the farm-road made a loop, and Bergview lay before them, like a picture postcard in the morning light.

This was how she would remember it, Jessica thought: the beautiful Cape Dutch house with its curved gables and the white walls that shone like marble in the sunshine; the garden surrounding the house, all old trees and flowering shrubs; the vineyards, green and purple against the distant mountains.

And then they were driving through the gates, and Kirk was turning the car on to the national road that led to Cape Town.

Jessica was relieved that Kirk kept the airport farewells to a minimum. Everything she wanted to say to Donny and Laura had already been said. She bent and hugged them to her. Laura was crying openly, and Jessica pretended not to notice that Donny's wet cheeks left damp spots against her own.

At last she straightened and looked at Kirk. His eyes were impersonal, his face without any expression. If he had thought at all about their kisses the night before there was nothing to show it. She stepped towards him, and his lips touched her cheek, briefly, politely.

'Have a good flight,' he said, then he took the hands of both children and led them away.

Jessica stood and watched them until they were out of sight in the crowds. She was relieved at the briefness of it all.

She also felt utterly deflated.

'...and they want to know when they can expect to have it. Jessica... *Jessica?*'

Jessica turned her head and focused her eyes on the man who stood by her drawing-board. She stared at her employer in a kind of daze, wondering how long he had been talking to her.

'Well, Jessica?'

'Stewart...' She shook her head. 'I'm sorry, I... Could you repeat the question, please?'

'I've asked it twice already, but you didn't hear me, did you?'

'I'm sorry...'

'Where were you?' His expression was a mixture of frustration and amusement. 'Don't tell me, I can guess. Bergview.'

'Is it so obvious?'

'You've talked of nothing but that wretched place in the two months you've been back. You mooch around the office looking distracted and oblivious of anyone who talks to you. My guess is that you dream about Bergview at night.'

'Sometimes,' she admitted.

'Do you miss the children so much?'

'Yes, I do. I worry about them. It's not as if they're alone. The housekeeper—Betty—is a gem, and she loves them both dearly. And then there's Kirk...' She stopped. When she went on, it was more grimly. 'But yes, I do worry about them.'

'Spoken to them lately?'

'Last night. I phone every few days. They seemed OK, but I can't help thinking...'

'What is it, Jessica?'

'I made a promise to Linda.'

'It's not your fault you couldn't keep it.'

'Maybe not... And yet I feel as if I've let down my sister and abandoned her children. I know that's silly. It isn't as if I didn't try everything I could to persuade Kirk to let me have them. Stewart...'

'Why do I get the feeling that you're about to say something I won't like?' He was eyeing her warily.

'I want to go back to Bergview.'

'You mean you want to take some more leave?'

'Not exactly.'

'You're not thinking of going there *permanently*?'

'I couldn't do that. It's Kirk's home, and he'd probably have a fit if he thought I was going to be there

forever. Especially not if he were to get married to...'
Again she stopped.

'I'm not sure what it is you're trying to say, Jessica?'

'I think I should hand in my notice.'

'That's ridiculous!'

'No...' She looked at him, her eyes troubled. 'I need to go back to Bergview, but I don't know how long I'll be there. That's why I want you to accept my notice, Stewart. Anything else wouldn't be fair to you.'

'When did you make this decision, Jess?'

'I'm not sure. I think it's been there, at the back of my mind, ever since I got back. And then last night, when I was talking to the children, I suddenly knew I had to be there with them.'

'When do you want to go?'

'It's Donny's birthday next Saturday. I'd really like to be there for that. Would it be an absolute nerve if I left you on Thursday, Stewart? That way I could catch a plane to Cape Town on Friday.'

'It won't be easy. You'll take some replacing, Jessica Bartlett; you're a damn good artist.'

'That's another thing—I'm going to need work.'

'You don't think Kirk would feed you?' There was a curious, speculative look in Stewart's eyes.

'I refuse to live on his charity,' Jessica said shortly.

'I see...'

'I was thinking... If I want to be with the children, a job like this would be the wrong thing for me. Do you think I could find some freelance work?'

'What exactly were you thinking of?'

'Illustrating of some kind. Book covers maybe, or magazine work.'

'Hmm...' He frowned thoughtfully. 'Say, you're good with flowers. How would you feel about doing some pictures for a calendar?'

'A *calendar*?' She looked at him eagerly.

'Do you remember Graham's, the pharmaceutical company? We did an advertising job for them some time ago.'

'Yes, of course I remember.'

'I was talking to Charles Graham just a few days ago. He's interested in putting out a personalised calendar for his customers. He was considering pictures of indigenous shrubs and flowers, and he asked me if I could recommend someone to do the drawing.'

'Stewart! Do you think you could get me the assignment?'

'I can try.'

'It would be ideal!' Jessica's eyes sparkled as she looked up at him.

'I'll see what I can do.'

'You're a darling, Stewart!'

'Actually, I think I'm a fool. We've had some good times together, Jessica. If I let you go to Bergview you may never come back.'

She put her hand on his arm. 'We *have* had good times, but that's all it's ever been. You know we've never been serious about each other.'

'We could have been—eventually. Jessica, what about this Kirk fellow?'

'Tom was his brother.'

'I know that, but I'm wondering what he is to you. Whenever you say his name there's a certain look in your eyes... I think I know you well enough to ask—are you in love with him?'

Jessica hesitated. Then she said, honestly, 'I'm not sure. Even if I did love him, it wouldn't do me any good. You see, there's someone else.'

'In that case, aren't you looking for a broken heart if you go back to Bergview?'

'Kirk has nothing to do with my decision,' she said firmly, 'I'm going because of a promise I made to my sister.'

CHAPTER FOUR

THE taxi was still some way from the house when Jessica spotted Kirk and the children in the distance. They were in the garden, but, perhaps because the winding farm road was sandy, they had not turned their heads at the sound of the vehicle.

Jessica sat forward in her seat. 'Please stop,' she said urgently.

'Here?' The driver looked at her in surprise. 'The house is further on.'

'Yes, I know it is, but this is where I want to get out.' Jessica smiled at the man's confusion. 'It's all right, I know what I'm doing.'

'What about the luggage, ma'am? How are you going to carry three suitcases?'

'You can leave them here, on the side of the road. They'll be taken care of.'

The driver shrugged, the look on his face revealing that he thought she was a little crazy. But he switched off the engine, got out of the vehicle, opened the boot and unloaded the suitcases.

When he saw the size of Jessica's tip, his expression lightened. 'You can always phone if you need a lift back to Cape Town, ma'am. Ask for William.' Evidently he had decided that she was not expected at Bergview.

Jessica waited till the taxi had gone before starting to walk in the direction of the garden. Her heart was beating a little too fast. William's supposition was correct. She was not expected. What if she was not welcome? If she really did have to summon William for a lift back to the airport?

She stopped among the trees that bordered the lush lawns. Kirk and the children were flying kites, and all of them had their backs to her. Kirk's kite was aloft, but Donny and Laura were having less success. They kept making small running spurts, but their kites dragged along the ground: at most, they rose an inch or two before flopping stubbornly back on to the grass.

'Looks as if you could do with a bit of help.'

Kirk had turned towards the children. He was laughing, and at the sight of his face, so zestful and vital and amused, Jessica felt her heart turn over. It was at that moment that she knew for certain that she was in love with him. She had suspected it for weeks—now there was no longer any doubt.

Watching him with the children, she could see how good he was with them—affectionate and warm and funny in a way she had never realised he could be. And they responded to him with an openness and trust which she would never have predicted two months ago.

With Kirk's help, Laura's kite rose into the air. She ran with it, calling out in glee. Donny's kite went up too, soaring as the wind caught it and played with it. Along the lawn he ran, with the kite lifting high behind him.

'Donald—the trees!' Kirk shouted. 'Hey, Don, boy, look out!'

But Donny, caught in the exhilaration of the moment, went on running. By the time he heard his uncle's voice, his kite had already come to grief in an oak tree.

'Uncle Kirk!' It was a confident shout rather than the stricken call Jessica expected. It was as if Donny knew without question that Kirk would help him. 'My kite's stuck!'

'Kites have a way of doing that.' Kirk was laughing. 'Let's get it down.'

Jessica tensed when she saw that Kirk intended Donny to bring the kite down himself. Instinctively she stepped forward, about to intervene before the little boy could

climb the tall tree and hurt himself. But she stopped
herself in time.

In seconds she realised that she need not have worried.
True, Donny was climbing the tree, but Kirk's hands
were always just at his feet, ready to steady him if he
stumbled, to catch him if he fell. When Donny jumped
down to the ground, kite in hand, face aglow with
triumph, it was clear that Kirk's way had been best.

Jessica took a breath. Then she walked out of the trees
and on to the lawn, calling, 'Any kites to spare for an
aunt?'

Three astonished faces turned her way, then Laura gave
a joyful cry and ran into her waiting arms. Donny stood
quite still a few seconds, then he came forward too and
let Jessica give him a kiss. Arms around them both, she
hugged them tightly.

And then, across their heads, she looked at Kirk. The
sun was behind him, gilding the dark tumbled hair and
making his eyes hard to read. For a long moment he did
not move. Oddly, he seemed more shocked than either
of the children.

'Kirk...' Jessica began, feeling less certain of her
welcome by the second.

'What a surprise,' he said at last.

'Well, yes...'

'We weren't expecting you, Jessica.'

'No, I know...'

'We didn't even see you arrive.'

'I got the taxi to drop me further down the drive, and
I walked from there.' Nerves had made her breathing
shallow, and she was talking too fast.

'Did you see me fly my kite, Aunt Jess?' asked Laura,
and at the same moment Donny said,

'Did you see me climb the tree?'

Her arms were still around them both. 'I saw you, and
you're both so clever. You'll have to teach me to fly a
kite too.'

'Look!' Donny said. Grabbing his kite, he ran along the lawn, while Laura ran after him.

Kirk waited till they were out of earshot, then he came closer to Jessica. 'This really is a surprise!'

He was just as she remembered him, tall and vital, so self-assured even now, when she had caught him off guard, still the most attractive man she had ever known.

'You must have planned to arrive in time for Donald's birthday tomorrow,' he said.

'Yes, I did.'

'Why didn't you let me know you were coming? I'd have fetched you from Cape Town.'

It was a question Jessica did not want to answer, so she changed the subject instead. 'I can't believe the change in Donny. He's not nearly so withdrawn any more.'

'Why didn't you phone, Jessica?'

'I saw how good you are with the children, Kirk. You've done wonders for them both.'

'I'm flattered,' he said drily. 'But you still haven't told me why you didn't let me know you were coming. You could have written or phoned. Why didn't you, Jessica? Are you going to tell me? Or do you intend changing the subject again?'

She made herself meet his gaze. 'I didn't know if I'd be welcome.'

'Well, how about that?' Something moved in the dark eyes that rested on her face. She wished she could read them.

'*Am* I welcome, Kirk?'

His hand went to her face, his fingers tracing a tantalising line down one cheek and around her lips. 'So you want to know if you're welcome, Jessica.'

'Am I?'

He laughed, the sound both mocking and sensuous as his warm breath fanned her face. 'What do *you* think?' he said then, turning the question back on her.

His touch, so long awaited, had set her heart pounding, so that she had to look away from him quickly lest her eyes betray her feelings. It was just as well that the children ran up at that moment, for she could not have given him an answer.

Long after the children had gone to bed and the house was in darkness, Jessica was awake. Through the open window came the shrilling of the crickets, and the warm air was heavy with the perfume of the shrubs that grew around the house.

Shifting restlessly beneath the sheets, Jessica wished she could sleep. But there was a sultriness in the vineyards that night that inflamed emotions still too raw from the morning's meeting with Kirk.

A swim—the idea came to her suddenly. In an instant she was out of bed and rummaging in her drawers for a bikini. She put it on quickly, then slipped jeans and a shirt over the top.

The house was in darkness as she stole out of her room and down the passage to the front door. One of the dogs barked as she opened the door, but she stilled it with a whisper. Very quietly she let the door close behind her.

The sky was clear and a half-moon lit the garden path, so that Jessica had no trouble finding her way in the dark. The pool was quite close to the house, but surrounded by shrubs. In the unlikely event of Kirk looking out of his window, he would not see her in the water.

Into the deep end she dived, and swam three lengths before she stopped at the edge of the pool and shook the wet hair out of her eyes. The water swished gently around her body. For the first time that day Jessica felt entirely at ease. Suddenly she laughed out loud.

'A mermaid!' A familiar voice was laughing too.

'Kirk!' Jessica tensed as she spun around. He was standing at the other end of the pool, his body naked apart from a swimsuit that was so tiny that he might almost have been wearing nothing at all.

'A mermaid with a joke to share?'

He was like some pagan god in the pale moonlight—virile, beautiful, infinitely sexier than any man had a right to be. Shoulders so broad above the narrow hips, thighs long and taut, calves and chest strongly muscled. There was not an inch of his body that did not proclaim male strength. As Jessica stared at him her own body tingled.

'Why were you laughing, Jessica?' The amusement was still in his voice, almost as if he knew the effect he was having on her. 'Are you going to share the joke with me?'

'It wasn't a joke,' she muttered unsteadily.

'But you were laughing, and I wondered why. A very beautiful laugh, incidentally. It sounded like music.'

Oh, but he knew how to talk sweetly, this man who was anything but sweet. He was tough and clever and fearless, ruthless when it suited him. He possessed all the qualities of a man who could hold his own in an intensely competitive world. And yet, with all that, he knew just how to seduce a girl with his looks and his words and his voice so that she became utterly vulnerable in his presence. Chances were he would be even more amused than he was already if he knew how she felt about him—Jessica, and a legion of other women. That was why she had to be on her guard with him.

Forcing her eyes away from the virile body, she said airily, 'If you must know, I was laughing because I was feeling good. After a long, hot day the water's wonderful.'

'Which is why I'm coming in to join you.'

A neat dive took him halfway across the pool with barely a splash to disturb the surface of the water. Seconds later he was at her side. He was laughing again, his teeth white and strong in the moonlight, his eyes sparkling. Without warning, he took hold of her hands and drew her away from the edge.

'Hey, Kirk!' she protested.

'Yes, Jessica?'

But it was too late to ask him what he was doing, for he had already propelled her to the centre of the pool. Stopping in a spot where it was too deep for Jessica to stand, he held her lightly beneath her elbows.

'You were right—the water really is wonderful tonight.' He was so close to her that even in the dark she could see the drops of water that clung to his lashes.

'I was about to get out,' she said.

'Liar. You've just got in.'

'I wanted to cool off, and I've done that.'

'Don't be so uptight, Jessica. Let's enjoy ourselves.'

'I don't think so, Kirk.'

But as she tried to swim away from him she found that though his hold on her elbows was light it was also firm. He had no intention of letting her go.

'I think I should go indoors now,' she said, as calmly as she was able.

'You want to get away from me,' he drawled.

After a moment, she said, 'What if I do?'

'I'm not ready to let you go, Jessica.'

Again she tested the hold on her arms. It was as firm as she'd suspected. A shiver shot through her, but it owed nothing to fear. Inside her, desire was hot and throbbing. She had not known she could want a man as much as she wanted Kirk.

'Why did you come to the pool?' she asked jerkily.

'What do you think?'

'I wish you wouldn't keep answering questions with more questions. Don't you know how maddening that is? I only know that the house was in darkness when I walked out. I thought everyone was asleep. Are you going to pretend it was coincidence that you decided to swim just when I was in the water?'

'I wouldn't say anything so stupid. Of course it wasn't coincidence, Jessica. I heard Bosco bark, I heard the front door close, and then I heard a splash and I knew you'd gone swimming.'

'You heard a splash?' she said disbelievingly. 'The pool isn't beneath your window.'

'Maybe you don't realise how far sound carries here at night.'

'Be that as it may,' she said scathingly, 'I suppose it never occurred to you that if I'd wanted company I could have knocked at your door?'

'Ah, but you wouldn't have done that, would you? Not the Jessica who tries so hard to put as much distance as she can between us—even though that's not at all what she really wants.'

His closeness and the tone of his voice were getting to her as much as the outrageousness of his words. She tried to push herself away from him, but her feet hit his calves, and before she could collect herself sufficiently to move again he had captured them between his legs.

She made herself look at him. 'Why *did* you come to the pool? The real reason, Kirk.'

'We've had no time alone together since you've been back. The children never leave your side for a moment. I need answers to some questions—questions I couldn't ask in front of Donald and Laura.'

The sensation of hard thighs against her feet was so erotic that it made her feel a little dizzy. 'If it's answers you're after, we can talk indoors,' she said. 'The children are asleep—they won't disturb us.'

'This is infinitely nicer,' Kirk said lazily, and pulled her closer against him.

The hairs of his chest brushed against the swell of her breasts where the skin was left bare by the curve of the bikini. Jessica was finding it harder and harder to breathe.

A little wildly, she said, 'I have a question too. I asked you earlier if I was welcome at Bergview, but you didn't answer me.'

She felt rather than heard the laughter in his throat. 'If you weren't welcome, don't you think I'd have told you?'

'That still isn't an answer, Kirk.'

'You've always been welcome at Bergview, Jessica, surely you know that. You're welcome now.'

'Because the children need someone to take care of them now that their parents are gone?'

It was a question that would have been much better left unasked, she knew that the moment the words had left her lips.

'There is that too,' Kirk said after a moment.

Which left Jessica feeling flat, even if it was the answer she had expected.

'My turn,' Kirk said then. 'How long are you staying this time?'

'I can't tell you exactly.'

'I need to know. Two weeks? Three?'

'You don't understand. I've given up my job. I can stay at Bergview as long as I like.'

She felt the stiffening of his body. 'How long exactly, Jessica?'

'As long as the children seem to need me.'

'*Well!*'

In the deep end of a swimming-pool, with a sexy man holding her against him, her feet clamped between his legs, it was almost impossible to think clearly, but Jessica tried. 'Is there a problem?'

'*You* don't think there is?'

'My board will cost you nothing, Kirk. I won't need to ask you for a cent. I've managed to line up some freelance artwork, and when I've finished it there'll be more.'

'I wasn't thinking of money, Jessica. Although I have to say you're an independent lady. Feisty too.'

'Are you saying there's another problem?'

'Isn't it obvious?' A thumb began a slow caressing movement on the soft inner skin of her upper arm as his legs tightened around her feet. 'I was talking of the sexy feelings that are between us all the time. Red-hot feelings, Jessica.'

Jessica swallowed. 'You're making too much of nothing.'

'Am I? You and I, living under one roof. Do you know what that will lead to?'

'It doesn't have to lead to anything at all,' Jessica said, trying to sound as if she meant it.

She loved Kirk, but she understood that she could not let herself be his plaything. A too available woman in his house, an easy convenience whenever he felt like a bit of fun. If that were to happen she would end up feeling cheap and used and bitter. She might even begin to hate him. So she must make an effort not to let him know quite how deeply he affected her.

'I wonder if you know what you're letting yourself in for, Jessica.'

'Sure I know,' she said. 'Now let me go.'

Once more she tried to push away from him, with all her strength this time. But in that moment both his arms tightened around her and he began to kiss her, deep, drugging kisses that shattered the resolve she had made just moments earlier, making it impossible to resist him.

Tremor after tremor shook her body as his mouth claimed hers, his tongue exploring the sweetness inside lips that seemed to have no choice but to part beneath his urging. One hand slid beneath her bikini bra to her breasts, the fingers cupping, caressing, teasing the nipples which became hard in moments. Jessica let out a moan of delight. The sound was involuntary, and for a moment she was able to hope it had never left her throat. Then Kirk lifted his head and she knew he had heard it.

For long seconds he looked down at her. His breathing was rough, and in the moonlight she saw an expression in his eyes which she had never seen there before. An odd expression, as if Kirk had caught a glimpse of something he had never expected.

'Let me go,' she whispered painfully. 'Please, Kirk, please let me go.'

He touched her face. 'I don't believe that's what you want.'

'I'm certain I want it.'

'Are you, Jessica?' he asked very softly. 'After what happened just now, I don't think you can be certain of anything.'

Next day they celebrated Donny's birthday.

It was too soon after the accident to have a big party with balloons and crackers and lots of noise. On the other hand, his aunt and uncle were determined he should enjoy the day.

It was one of those lovely Cape mornings when the sky was blue and cloudless over the vineyards, and it was impossible to believe that anyone, given the chance, would want to spend the day indoors. Betty packed a picnic lunch, and when the children were out of the way Jessica and Kirk packed the boot of the car with gift-wrapped presents.

'So, birthday boy, where shall we picnic?' asked Kirk.

Donny thought for a moment. 'Can we go to the beach?'

'Good idea,' said his uncle. 'It's just the day for it.'

An hour later they were in Fish Hoek, on the other side of Table Mountain from the turbulent Atlantic waters where Linda and Tom had come to grief.

A fishing-boat was pulling in at the pier just as Jessica and Kirk and the children came down to the beach. Donny and Laura dropped their buckets and spades on the sand and ran to the boat, where already people were crowding round to see the fishermen unload their catch.

Kirk grinned at Jessica. 'How's that for good timing? Should be a while before they come back. Gives us a chance to get the party organised.'

Jessica laughed back at him. 'Good timing indeed. I was wondering how we were going to manage with the kids hanging around.'

Shading her eyes, she watched Donny and Laura bending eagerly over the fish. 'Isn't it strange, I'd have thought the ocean and the boat might be more than they could deal with. It's not long since...'

Kirk shot her a look. 'I don't think they associate the fishing-boat with the one their parents drowned in. It doesn't mean they've forgotten.'

'No...'

'I found Laura weeping in her sleep a few nights ago. And Donald cries now and then, when he's quite certain nobody's watching him.'

'Poor babies, if only there was something we could do for them,' Jessica said painfully.

'You've made them both very happy simply by coming back to them,' he said, and the look in his eyes, even more than his words, brought a flush of pleasure to Jessica's cheeks.

A few minutes later Donny and Laura came racing back along the sand. Laura's fair hair was a windblown halo round her elfin face, and Donny's eyes sparkled with excitement. The fish were *huge*, they said, bigger than any fish Betty had ever bought at the market. Bet they tasted better too.

Jessica and Kirk exchanged a smile. They had made the most of their time. The gifts were concealed beneath a pile of towels where the children would not think of looking for them.

'It's years since I made a sand-castle,' Jessica said. 'Do I have any helpers?'

Both children were eager to help, and Kirk joined in too. Near the edge of the water, where the outgoing tide had left the sand hard and wet, a castle was soon taking shape. When it had reached its full height, Donny and Laura went off to hunt for shells, leaving Jessica and Kirk to dig a tunnel.

Working at opposite sides, with the grit scraping beneath their fingernails, they tunnelled away. Quite suddenly their fingers met. One moment there was sand separating their hands, the next the last barrier was down and their fingers were touching.

And then a long finger hooked itself around a smaller one. Another finger tickled the palm of a soft hand. Across the top of the castle, Jessica laughed at Kirk, but the sparkle in her eyes came from an inner excitement.

'You really are a bit of a rogue,' she told him.

'A rogue and a castle.' His eyes were sparkling too—a particularly wicked sparkle—as he tickled her again. 'You do know, don't you, Jessica, that all the best rogues keep ladies in their castles?'

'Oh, really?'

'Certainly. Only the most beautiful ladies, enormously sexy.'

'How nice for the rogues,' she said lightly, playing along with his teasing.

'Would you say we fit the bill, Jessica? A rogue and his gorgeous lady?'

'What do *you* say?'

'Since we've established what I am—and since you are one very tantalising lady—I'd have to say yes.'

'Do you flirt with every woman you meet, Kirk?'

'That's for you to decide.'

She looked at him across the sand-castle, at gold-flecked eyes that shone in the sun, at sensuous lips that could wreak havoc with riotous senses, at arms that were muscled and tanned and made a girl forget everything but their strength when they folded around her body, and she wished she could separate truth from teasing, and flirtatiousness from real feelings.

'Well, Jessica?'

'Yes, I think you're a flirt, Kirk.' She forced herself to hide her hopes and her doubts as she laughed into his face.

'Only a flirt, Jessica?'

'I've hardly had time to find out if there's more to you than that.'

'Maybe you should give yourself the time.'

'Maybe,' she said, and was glad when the children came back just then with their buckets filled with shells. Kirk unhooked her finger and she was able to withdraw her hand from the tunnel.

The castle was decorated with shells and pebbles and garlands of seaweed. Kirk took photos of the children kneeling beside it, and everyone declared it the very best castle ever built.

The big moment came after the picnic lunch. Betty had thought of everything—hot dogs and tomato sauce and crisp salty chips; lemonade and lollipops and a birthday cake with six candles. When the last crumbs of the cake had been eaten, with a flourish worthy of a magician, Kirk pulled the towels away from the pile of parcels.

Laura gave a squeal of delight, while Donny's eyes widened with surprise. It did not take the little boy long to open his presents. From Kirk there was a model aeroplane and a soccer ball, from Jessica a paintbox and a sketch-pad. There was also a teddy-bear. Jessica had given much thought to this last present, wondering if Donny would consider himself too old for a teddy. And then she had thought of the small, tense, unhappy child, alone with his grief in the night, and had decided to give in to her instincts. She and Linda had held on to torn and shabby bears long after they had discarded their other toys; perhaps Donny would find a measure of comfort in his own teddy-bear.

For all that the birthday was Donny's, Laura had not been forgotten. Kirk, who knew how much his little niece loved stories, had bought her a thick book of bedside tales. 'You can have a story every night,' he promised. From Jessica there was a bear just like Donny's, which Laura immediately hugged to her chest.

Towards the end of the day Kirk and the children went in the water for one last swim. Jessica had already changed into her jeans and shirt, and she watched them from the sand.

'What a lovely family you have!'

Jessica turned in surprise to an elderly woman who had been sitting not far away from them.

'I couldn't help watching you. The little girl is the image of you, isn't she? And the boy takes after your husband. What a handsome man he is—and so much in love with you!'

Jessica opened her mouth to tell the woman she had it all wrong—that Kirk did not love her, nor were they a family. But at that moment the woman stood up and began to shake the sand out of her possessions. With a smile and a friendly goodbye she was gone, leaving Jessica to stare after her.

Kirk and the children returned from their swim a few minutes later, and Jessica forgot the woman's comments as she threw towels round both children and rubbed them dry.

By the time they left the beach and piled into the car, the sun was setting over the mountains and the sea. Donny and Laura, tired after the long day, were quiet on the drive back to the estate.

'Are they sleeping?' Kirk asked after a while.

Jessica glanced over her shoulder. 'Soundly. They won't wake up till we get back home.'

It was almost dark when Kirk turned off the national road and drove through the gates of Bergview. Parked outside the house was a sporty-looking Porsche.

'Alicia,' said Kirk, and Jessica thought he sounded surprised.

A moment later the door of the house opened and Alicia appeared. 'Darling!' she called as Kirk got out of the car. 'I've been waiting here for hours!'

Jessica got out of the car then and Alicia's eyes narrowed in disbelief.

'So,' she hissed, 'you're back! Pretending to be the concerned aunt again. Is that why I had no part in Donald's birthday?'

CHAPTER FIVE

'DID we have an arrangement, Alicia?' Kirk looked puzzled as they walked up the steps and sat down on the veranda.

Alicia hesitated. 'Not exactly... But I'd thought all along that it would be nice to do something special to celebrate Donald's birthday.'

'If only you'd said so! We spent the day on the beach. We could so easily have all gone together.'

The children, still a little sleepy-looking after the drive home, flinched. Alicia threw Jessica a vicious look, but when she turned back to Kirk she was smiling.

'Beach parties aren't exactly my scene, darling—after all these years you must know that. Actually, Mother and I had something else in mind. A bit of a party at our house.'

'I didn't know that,' said Kirk.

'Mother was even more disappointed than I was. She just took it for granted we'd be seeing you, and she spent so much time baking a few special treats for the children. Did you know there was a puppet show in Paarl? I'd been thinking all week that we might take Donald and Laura to see it.'

Jessica glanced at the children, who looked anything but sorry that the day had turned out so differently from the way Alicia had planned it. Though she did not particularly like the other woman, Jessica could not help but empathise with her disappointment.

In a friendly tone, she stopped them as they were about to go indoors. 'Laura... Donny... why don't you stay out here with Uncle Kirk and Miss Mason? I'll go and get us some cake and something cool to drink.'

In the kitchen, Betty was ironing. As Jessica cut up a fruit cake and prepared a jug of ice-cold lemonade, she told the housekeeper how good the picnic lunch had been, and how excited the children had been with the birthday cake.

Betty was delighted. 'They need more treats. It's a good thing you came back to Bergview, Miss Jess.'

'I hope you're right, Betty.'

'I am right. The children will be OK with you and Mr Kirk.'

Jessica was smiling as she carried the tray out of the kitchen. On the veranda, she stopped in surprise. Masses of torn gift paper littered the floor. Donny, his cheeks flushed with excitement, was ringing the bell of a brand-new bicycle. It was all shiny chrome and bright red metal and had a matching red pennant attached to the handlebars.

'You shouldn't have done this, Alicia,' Kirk was saying, and Jessica saw that his eyes were troubled.

But Alicia was unperturbed by his reaction as she produced another gift-wrapped parcel.

'For you, Laura, dear,' she smiled.

The parcel was huge, as big as the child. Laura studied it warily for a few seconds before proceeding to tear open the paper.

There was a gasp from Donny and a cry from Laura as Alicia lifted a doll out of a cardboard box—a doll that was almost as tall as Laura. It had golden curls and a pouting pink mouth, and it could walk and talk and cry.

Laura looked stunned, while Donny looked awed. Jessica felt a little empty. Her own gifts, so happily given, were as nothing beside Alicia's offerings.

'You shouldn't have done this, Alicia,' Kirk said again.

'Nonsense, darling!'

'It's far too much.'

'How can anything be too much?' Alicia gave a tinkling laugh. 'The children and I are going to be friends, after all—*very good friends*. Aren't we, darlings?' Her voice was weighted with meaning.

There was a small silence as everyone looked at her.

'And if you think the day was spoiled for me, then you're mistaken.' Alicia's voice was as merry as ever. 'The puppet show is still on tomorrow. What say we go in the afternoon? Right, Kirk?'

'Sure, why not?'

'Wonderful! I'll get four tickets.'

Jessica stared at Alicia, her breath taken away by the deliberateness of the slight.

'Five tickets,' corrected Kirk, with a look at Jessica.

'Five—good heavens, how silly of me! Somehow I imagined Jessica would have things to do—having only just arrived at Bergview, I mean—but it doesn't matter, I can get five tickets just as easily.'

Jessica had recovered her composure by this time. 'Make it four, Alicia,' she said lightly.

'Jessica . . . ?' Kirk was looking at her again.

Jessica looked past him at Alicia, whose watchful eyes were narrowed and hard. 'Alicia's right,' she said, still in the same light voice, 'I do have things to do. I'll be glad to have some time to myself.'

Jessica was sitting on the veranda the next afternoon, sketching a protea, when the sporty little Porsche came tearing up the drive. The children hopped out, followed, seconds later, by Alicia.

'Kirk asked to be dropped by the lower vineyards,' she said abruptly, in answer to Jessica's questioning look.

'Well, and did you all have a good time?' asked Jessica.

'Sort of,' Laura said, while Donny muttered,

'It was OK.'

'You'll have to tell me about it,' Jessica said.

'Later,' Alicia said tersely. She had been holding a bakery packet which she now gave to Donny. 'Take this to the kitchen, Donald. You can have what's left of these buns for your tea tomorrow or whenever. Go with him, Laura.'

The children vanished readily. Alicia jerked a chair from the table and sat down. Jessica put down her pencil.

'Was the show fun?' she asked, in as friendly a tone as she was able to summon.

'Fantastic! Wonderful,' Alicia said, in the kind of voice people normally used to describe something awful.

Jessica sat back quietly and wondered what was bothering the other woman. She did not have long to wait for the answer.

'So you decided to come back to Bergview.' The husky seductiveness Alicia used when she spoke to Kirk was missing from her tone.

'That's right.'

'When I saw you yesterday I thought you'd only come back for Donald's birthday, but Kirk tells me it's an extended visit this time.'

'You could say that.'

'How long, Jessica?'

'I can't tell you. As long as I feel I'm needed. Didn't Kirk tell you that too?'

'Something to that effect—that you'd given up your job to be with the kids. That you're going to be doing freelance art of some kind.' Moodily, Alicia reached for the roughly pencilled protea and pulled it towards her. 'Is this what you're working on?'

'Yes, it is. It's going to be an illustration for a calendar of wildflowers.'

'*This* is how you intend to earn a living? Because I take it you don't expect Kirk to support you?'

'No, I don't, though I think that's a matter between Kirk and myself, don't you?'

Alicia gave one of her hard stares before turning back to the sketch. 'This flower doesn't look the kind of thing people will pay money for.'

'I hope they will when it's finished.'

'Even if they do, it won't be enough to keep you clothed and fed.'

'I think you're trying to say something, Alicia.'

Abruptly Alicia pushed the pad away from her. 'I want to know—are you after Kirk?'

'You can't be serious, asking me a question like that.' Jessica looked at her with distaste.

'*Are you?*'

'Don't be silly!'

'If it's not Kirk, then what's it all about? A cushy life at Bergview?'

'It would be best if you didn't go on with this, Alicia.'

'Perhaps you see yourself as a substitute for the children's mother?'

Jessica was suddenly very angry. 'I'm their aunt, nothing else.'

'Right! But has it ever occurred to you that Kirk might see you as a mother figure?'

'I can't say it has.'

'How could you not? Your being here makes it all so easy for him. He keeps his brother's children at Bergview while Linda's mirror image looks after them. What could be more convenient?'

'If that's what Kirk thinks, then that's his affair, isn't it?'

'So then you really are determined to stay?'

'For the moment.'

'Kirk cares nothing at all for you on a personal level, Jessica.'

'Since my being here has nothing to do with Kirk, I can't see that it matters what he feels about me,' Jessica managed to say coolly.

Alicia stood up, smoothing down her red leather skirt with perfectly manicured hands. At the top of the steps she turned.

'I do have one warning, Jessica. Don't get yourself too ingrained here at Bergview. Things can change very quickly, I hope you know that.'

'Things can always change, Alicia.'

Jessica kept a smile on her face as the beautiful woman walked quickly and angrily back to her car, but, in the palms of her hands, her nails dug painfully into her soft skin.

It was about a month later that the man appeared. Jessica was sitting in the garden, her head bent over her sketchpad, so absorbed in her work that she did not hear him coming up behind her. Only when his shadow fell across the paper did she look up.

He was quite old, and a little shabby in run-down *veldskoene* and overalls which had long since lost their colour. On his head was a hat that looked as if it lived permanently on his long, matted grey hair, and a mottled white beard reached from his chin halfway down his chest.

Stopping in front of Jessica, he doffed his hat. 'I've come to see Mr Kirk.'

'I'm afraid Kirk isn't at home,' she said.

Kirk was in France. His abrupt return to Bergview at the time of the accident had meant cutting short his business in the French vineyards. It was business he had had to get back to. He had been gone ten days, and Jessica missed him more than she cared to admit to herself.

In the month since she had come back to Bergview, life had settled into a routine of sorts. Kirk went about his business, rising earlier than anyone else in the house, out in the wineries or in his office before Jessica had driven the children to school. She spent as much time as she could with the children, and found herself growing closer to them every day. But Donny was in grade one now, and Laura was at nursery school, so in the mornings Jessica was alone. This was *her* time, the time she spent researching, sketching, painting.

There were times when they were all together—dinner, usually, and weekends, when they would plan special outings and fun activities. Jessica would look from Kirk to Donny and Laura, and she would feel there were ways in which they were very nearly the family the woman on the beach had taken them to be. But there were also times when Kirk was away from home in the evenings, when he went out—with Alicia?—and then Jessica would be reminded that they were not a family at all.

He would be gone for another week at least.

'Are you and the children all right?' he had asked last night—as he had every night since he had been away.

'We're fine.' Jessica had smiled into the telephone. She had been waiting all day for this call. 'It's amazing— your voice sounds just as clear as if we were in the same room talking.'

'The marvels of modern technology!' Kirk laughed. 'We really could be in the same room. Which is why you have only to let me know if there's anything that concerns you. There's not much I can't deal with from here.'

'There's nothing that needs your special attention,' she had reassured him, warmed by his concern.

In the garden, the bearded man was looking at her thoughtfully. 'When will Mr Kirk be back?'

Jessica hesitated. 'I'm not certain,' she said then, reluctant to tell a stranger more than she had to.

'Tonight?'

'No, I don't think so.'

His forehead creased in such deep furrows that Jessica offered, 'Maybe *I* can help you?'

'Maybe...' He peered at her from beneath the brim of his hat. 'In two days' time I'm going up the mountain.'

'The mountain?'

'There...' He gestured. 'Into the *kloof*. The little boy is coming with me.'

'*Donny?*'

'Yes, miss. I aim to leave at sunrise. Can he be ready at six?'

The sketch-pad dropped to the ground as Jessica stood up. 'Donny isn't going anywhere, Mr... Look, I don't even know your name.'

'Marius—Marius Theron. Mr Kirk knows about it. He said it would be OK.'

'There must be some mistake, Mr Theron.'

'No mistake. It was all arranged, miss. Maybe Mr Kirk forgot to tell you.'

Jessica's sensibilities screamed at her to tell Marius Theron to leave. And yet, despite the sudden element of danger, there was something open and honest and rather appealing about the old man. Something that made her continue talking to him when she could have sent him away.

'How long will you be in the *kloof*, Mr Theron?'

'Two days, maybe three.'

'Well, then, you must see how impossible it would be for Donny to come with you. He's a child. He's only six years old!'

'He is not too young to camp, to learn about the birds and the animals.'

'I'm sorry,' she said, 'but it's really out of the question.'

'The child will be upset, miss.'

'Donny doesn't know anything about this. I'm sure he would have told me about it if he did.'

'Maybe Mr Kirk was keeping it a surprise.'

'Maybe... But in any case, I can't allow it. I'm sorry, Mr Theron.'

'Maybe you can phone Mr Kirk. Ask him... He will tell you what has been arranged.'

Jessica hesitated a moment. It would be easy enough to mention Marius Theron on the telephone tonight. She and Kirk could discuss the fact that he wanted to take Donny into the mountains.

But no! There was nothing to discuss. Even if Kirk had in some crazy moment led this strange old man to believe that he could take their nephew camping, she could not allow it. There was no way she would even think of allowing Donny to go on an expedition of this kind. If something terrible happened to Linda's child, she would never forgive herself.

Gently, she said, 'I'm sorry, Mr Theron, but it really isn't possible.'

'I'm sorry too, miss.'

There was a look of disappointment in the old man's eyes. But he said nothing more as he doffed his cap once more and walked away.

Jessica was up very early the day Kirk came home. A few hours from now the plane would be landing in Cape Town. He would take a cab from the airport, he had said.

Shivering a little in the chill of pre-dawn, she sipped a mug of warm coffee as she stood at the kitchen window and looked outside. Mist lay over the valley and in the distance the mountains were no more than an indistinct blur. By the time Kirk arrived the mist would have vanished and the vineyards would be green and purple in the midday sun.

Jessica turned as Laura, huddled in fluffy yellow pyjamas, came into the kitchen.

'You're up early, honey.' Jessica bent to kiss her little niece.

'I'm too excited to sleep. Are you excited, Aunty Jess?'

'Yes, I am.' The calmness of Jessica's voice hid the tumult of her emotions. She felt as if she could not wait even one more hour to see Kirk again.

On the spur of the moment she made up her mind. 'Would you like to go and fetch Uncle Kirk from the airport?'

'*Can we?*' Laura looked ecstatic.

'I don't see why not. It's Saturday, so there's no school today. Let's wake Donny, and we'll have an early breakfast.'

They made such good time that they were at the airport long before the plane touched down. Expectantly, they hovered near the arrival doors.

People moved forward suddenly as the passengers came walking through the doors. The children craned their heads, peering impatiently, and Jessica picked Laura up so that the little girl could see better.

Suddenly there he was, walking rapidly through the crowd—tall, and so good-looking, with a vibrancy, even now when he was tired, that set him apart from all the other passengers. Jessica felt her heart do an odd little somersault as she stared at him.

Laura wriggled out of Jessica's arms, and she and Donny ran to meet Kirk.

Clearly, he had not been expecting them. He paused in mid-step, his face amazed. 'Uncle Kirk!' the children cried, and he lifted them up, one in each arm, and kissed them.

And then he had put them down and was looking at Jessica. She had not moved since the moment she had seen him.

'Jessica...' He came over to her, and she saw the warmth in his eyes. 'It's good to see you.'

'It's good to see you too, Kirk.'

Tame words to express the fact that it was pretty darn terrific that he was back.

'I thought I'd told you I'd take a taxi.'

She smiled at him. 'You did tell me, but the children and I thought this would be nicer.'

'It's very nice indeed.'

He touched her then, a feather-light caress of his fingers running from the corners of her lips to her eyes. And it did not matter that he had not kissed her.

'Were you surprised to see us? Were you surprised, Uncle Kirk?' the children kept asking as they made their way to the car.

'More surprised than I can tell you. Hey, what do you think? Shall we go and have something nice to eat before we drive back to Bergview?'

Once more he looked at Jessica. And once more the wonderful warm look was in his eyes.

Jessica was baking when she heard Kirk striding through the house a few days later. It was early afternoon, a time when he was usually in the vineyards.

She turned to him gladly as he appeared in the doorway of the kitchen. It was a moment before she saw the anger in his face.

'We have to talk.' He bit out the words.

'Kirk...?' she said uncertainly.

'Not in here.'

'Kirk, what is it? The children! Has something happened to one of the children?'

'*Come along*, Jessica!'

She wiped floury hands that were suddenly trembling. In the mixing bowl the baking-powder would go flat, but she did not give that a thought as she followed him down the passage and into his study.

'You have to tell me what's wrong,' she said. 'Don't keep me in suspense like this!'

'You're the one with some talking to do, Jessica.'

'I don't understand...'

'Marius dropped by the vineyards this morning.'

'Marius...? Oh, Marius! Marius Theron?'

'That same Marius,' he said grimly. 'Are things any clearer now?'

'He told you I didn't let Donny go into the mountains with him.'

'He did indeed.'

'He *couldn't* have thought I would say yes!'

'Certainly he did.'

'That's ridiculous! What about you, Kirk? Did you really think I'd let Donny go off with some stranger?'

'Marius is one of the kindest, wisest people I've ever known. Now he's disappointed and hurt. How could you do it to him, Jessica? Especially when it was all arranged.'

'You didn't tell me a thing about it.'

He frowned. 'I didn't? Are you sure?'

'Absolutely. Do you think I wouldn't have remembered a thing like that?'

'All right, then, maybe I didn't tell you. I had a lot on my mind at the time—problems with the vineyards, the trip to France.'

'Yet you blame me for not knowing. I don't happen to have psychic powers, Kirk.'

'I'm sorry. I should have told you. But even then . . . Once Marius told you it had been arranged, you could have asked me about it. There wasn't a night I didn't phone you.'

'I did think of mentioning it,' Jessica admitted.

'Why didn't you? We could have talked about it.'

'Because when I thought about it, I realised there was nothing to talk about.'

'I would have told you what Marius and I had planned for Donald.'

'Even if you had told me, Kirk, I wouldn't have let Donny go up that mountain.'

'I don't believe what I'm hearing, Jessica! You would actually have gone against what I'd arranged?'

There was something particularly autocratic in the lifting of the heavy eyebrows. Kirk was not accustomed to being contradicted or crossed, Jessica thought.

'Yes, I would have gone against you,' she said firmly.

'Why?'

'Because Donny's six years old. He's much too young to be wandering about in dangerous terrain.'

'Dangerous terrain indeed!' Kirk gave a short laugh. 'Marius Theron knows every inch of the mountains. Donald would have come to no harm with him.'

'I wouldn't have let him go.'

Kirk's tone was scathing. 'Don't tell me you were concerned because Donald wouldn't be having a bath for a few days? Or because he might not have got to bed on time?'

'I'm not neurotic, Kirk. What worried me was the loneliness of the *kloof*. Donny and one fragile old man. Think of it, Kirk. There are wild animals up there, for one thing. Or Donny could have slipped and fallen. Anything could have happened!'

'Marius knows what he's about. He's an experienced woodsman.'

'Maybe he is, but I still say Donny's too young for an expedition of this sort.'

'I was younger than Donald when Marius took me into the mountains the first time. Did he tell you that?'

'He said something,' she said cautiously.

'He taught me how to make a camp-fire and how to pitch a tent. He showed me the tracks of those wild animals you're so scared of, and I learned how to survive if ever I was lost. Those are things a boy remembers all his life, Jessica. I've never forgotten my trips with Marius Theron.'

Looking at Kirk, Jessica tried to picture him as a young boy, tanned and dark-haired and alert even then, enraptured with the thrill of new experiences, and something softened inside her.

'I suppose it would have made an impression,' she said slowly.

'Meaning you won't deprive Donald of the experience next time?'

'He can go when he's older.'

'I'm talking about now—at this point. The next time Marius Theron decides to go on a trip.'

The softness vanished as Jessica's defences went up. 'No, Kirk. No way! I would never allow it.'

'Don't you want to see Donald grow into a man, Jessica?'

'Of course I do. But he'll do that anyway, without you thrusting him into danger before he can handle it.'

'You haven't understood a word I've said, have you?'

'I understand that I'm the children's aunt. I understand that I have to make decisions I can live with.'

'Do you also understand that I'm their uncle?'

'Of course...'

'As well as their guardian,' he drawled.

Jessica swallowed. 'You're *not* going to pull that one on me, Kirk!'

'I'm reminding you that legally I make decisions for Donald and Laura.'

She had not known that you could love a man and yet be terribly angry with him at the same time.

'Certain decisions,' she said carefully, making an effort to remain calm. 'Where the children will live, how their finances are regulated—that sort of thing. As for the rest, now that I'm at Bergview, anything that affects their daily lives is *my* concern.'

'That's not the way I see it.'

'Are you telling me it will always be this way, Kirk? Will you veto all the decisions I make?'

'If I disagree with them.'

'What if I can't live with that?'

Kirk was silent.

'Maybe there isn't room for two substitute parents at Bergview,' Jessica said at last.

'Maybe not.'

Her throat had become so dry that it was difficult to talk. The colour had left her cheeks and her eyes were wide and shocked.

'Are you asking me to leave, Kirk?'

He was almost as pale as she was, but she was too distraught to notice. For a long moment he did not speak. Then he said, 'I'm not saying anything of the sort.' Before she could make anything of that, he added, 'Only *you* can decide what you should do, Jessica.'

The first light of dawn was beginning to penetrate the darkness, and still Jessica was awake. A day and most of a night had passed since her confrontation with Kirk, and she was no nearer a solution. On the one hand, she did not know if she could tolerate Kirk's arrogance. The fact that she loved him only seemed to make his arrogance worse somehow. On the other hand, there was her promise to Linda. How—*in heaven's name, how*— could she abandon the children?

Abruptly she jumped out of a bed that was rumpled from hours of tossing and turning. Thrusting her arms through her gown, she left the room and made for the kitchen. Maybe if she made herself something warm to drink she would feel a little better, more able to think clearly and come to a decision.

To Jessica's surprise, the light was on in the kitchen. For a moment she wondered if she had forgotten to switch it off before she went to bed. And then she saw Kirk.

Half lying, half sitting, he was fast asleep on the little two-seater by the big bay window, a half-empty coffee-mug on the floor by his feet. His face was pale and a little drawn, and long eyelashes threw slanting shadows on cheeks that were rough with early-morning stubble.

For a long moment Jessica stood in the doorway watching him. Then, very quietly, making sure her slippers made no sound on the stone floor, she went to him.

This was a Kirk she had never seen before. No trace of arrogance in him now. In his sleep he was vulnerable and defenceless. A shiver went through him, and for a moment his face contorted in a grimace. His arms, where the skin was bare, had a slight goose-pimply look, and when she touched his hand she found that the skin was cold. She wondered how long he had been there.

A smile touched her lips and her eyes as she watched him. She wanted nothing more than to wrap her arms around his cold body and keep him warm. An insane desire if ever there was one, given the fact that Kirk would repulse her if he were to wake up and find her so close to him.

At least there was one thing Jessica could do. In the bottom of the cupboard in her room there was an eiderdown, folded and ready for winter. She fetched it. When she came back into the kitchen, Kirk was still sleeping.

She covered him gently. One of his arms was flung sideways over the edge of the two-seater, and she lifted it, carefully, so as not to waken him, and folded it under the eiderdown.

For a few seconds longer she stood watching him. He had not moved, had given no sign of waking. It was even colder than she had realised, and she was beginning to shiver herself by now. Wrapping her dressing-gown more closely around herself, she walked towards the door.

'Jessica.' She heard her name as she was about to leave the kitchen.

She turned. Kirk was still in exactly the same position. Only his half-open eyes showed that he was awake.

'I thought you were sleeping.'

'I was.'

'Go back to sleep, then. I'm on my way to bed myself.'

'Don't go.'

'Is there something I can get you? A cup of warm milk?'

Kirk chuckled. It was the nicest sound Jessica had heard in a long while.

'Warm milk, indeed! Do you think you're talking to the kids now, Jessica? A strong cup of coffee with a good lacing of brandy is a drink for a cold man.'

'I don't know where you keep the brandy, but I don't mind making you some coffee,' she said.

'I'll settle for that if you'll have it with me.'

Jessica hesitated.

'Just a cup of coffee, Jessica. Afterwards you can go back to being silent and angry with me.'

She laughed. 'You say the darnedest things, don't you, Kirk Lemayne?'

'If I can make you laugh it's worth it. Never mind a laugh, I haven't heard so much as a word from you since yesterday morning.'

'You haven't been too talkative yourself,' she reminded him.

'Maybe not. Time to remedy the situation.'

'I think you're right,' Jessica agreed.

When the coffee was made, she carried him a mug. Then she sat down at the kitchen table with her own drink.

'Not there,' he said.

'I'm comfortable here.'

'Your toes are turning blue.'

'You must have X-ray eyes if you can see my toes through my slippers!'

'One of my lesser-known attributes—didn't you know?' he said, and she laughed again.

'Come here.' He held out an arm.

'I don't think so, Kirk.'

'I won't lay a finger on you—not that I wouldn't like to, of course—I promise.'

'My toes are fine just where they are.'

'You'd be a lot more comfortable if you sat here with me.'

She was so tempted, so incredibly tempted. 'No,' she said, and in her own ears her tone lacked conviction.

His arms were long. His hand reached for hers, taking her wrist, drawing her up from her chair. 'Come on, Jessica.'

'Well, maybe...' She gave in. 'Just while I drink this coffee.'

She thought he would push the eiderdown aside so that she could sit down beside him. Instead, he lifted up the corner and motioned to her to get beneath it.

'No, Kirk.'

'I made you a promise.'

'We're not exactly friends at the moment, remember?'

'I thought we'd agreed on a truce. Just until we finish our coffee?'

His eyes were fully open now and sparkling with mischief. It was an invitation Jessica could not resist. When he spread the eiderdown over her, she did not have the will-power to move away.

Moments later, seated beside Kirk under the thick down cover, she realised she had been very stupid. The poor icy body she had taken such pity on earlier seemed to have revived with astonishing speed. It had a warmth and a vibrancy which brought all her senses to throbbing life.

'Coffee OK?' she asked briskly, determined not to let things get out of hand. She would drain her mug quickly, then she would leave the kitchen and return to the safety—and the utter boredom—of her own room.

Kirk took a sip. 'Excellent,' he pronounced, then put his mug down as if he was in no hurry to finish it.

It was important to keep the conversation going.

'How long have you been sitting here, Kirk?'

'I'm not sure. An hour, maybe longer. I don't really know. I'd been lying awake and I thought I'd make myself something to drink.'

'I noticed the cold coffee.'

'Which I didn't finish in the end. Not as good as yours, I suppose. I must have dozed off.'

'Is there something on your mind, Kirk?' She asked the question out of a concern she could not seem to help.

'A few things. None of them very serious.'

'If you want to talk...' she suggested.

'There are a few problems with the estate right now. Nothing that can't be solved, just things I have to take care of.'

'I suppose there's much more for you to do now that Tom's not here.'

'Right.'

'Can you manage alone?'

'Oh, sure, I will. I have to.'

So optimistically spoken. But Bergview was a huge concern, Jessica knew. Bearing the sole responsibility for running the estate could not be easy.

'Actually,' Kirk added, 'I'm more concerned about the children than I am about Bergview. Donald is so much better now than he was at the beginning, but there are times when I see a terrible sadness. And Laura misses her mother.'

'You really do care about the children, don't you?'

'You sound surprised, Jessica. You must know I love them. I've said so often enough.'

'I do know you love them,' she said quietly.

He put an arm around her shoulders, and her body stiffened. If he noticed, he made no comment.

'Would it make a difference if I asked you not to leave?' he asked after a while.

She turned to look at him, and saw that the last of the mischief had left his face. 'I didn't think it would matter to you if I left. You said——'

'I know what I said, Jessica. Actually, I think we both said some things in the heat of the moment which we regretted afterwards.'

'Maybe we did...'

'Have you been lying awake trying to make a decision, Jessica? Is that why you came to the kitchen when you should have been sleeping?'

'Actually... Yes, I was thinking about what I should do,' she said, as calmly as she could.

'And what did you decide?'

'I haven't. Not yet.'

'I hope you'll stay.'

She was not yet ready to give him an answer.

'What happened with Marius Theron... Kirk, nothing has changed since we argued yesterday morning. I still think you're trying too hard to push Donny into independence.'

'And I think you're trying too hard to build a protective wall round him.'

'See?' she said. 'It's obvious it can't work. We're arguing again.'

'No, we're not. We're *talking*. There's a difference.'

'We think so differently, Kirk.'

'You're forgetting something—the most important thing. We both love the children.'

'Yes...'

'Even parents don't always have the same ideas.'

'That's true.'

'Will you give it another try, Jessica?'

It was what she wanted to do.

'Jessica?'

She closed her eyes.

'Well, Jessica?'

'Maybe I will,' she said. 'For a while, anyway... For the sake of the children.'

After a moment Kirk said, 'For the sake of the children. Of course.' His voice was a little flat.

Silence fell after that. They sat close together, drinking their coffee. Jessica was filled with a happiness that spread right through her and warmed her as no eiderdown could do. Just the thought of leaving Kirk and the children had torn at her heart.

It had been growing lighter as they talked. At last Jessica said, 'Time we went to bed.'

'*Together*, Jessica? Did you really say that?'

'Idiot!' She laughed through the hard pulse in her throat. 'Each to our own bed. To rescue a little of what's left of the night.'

'Pity.'

She was pushing aside the eiderdown when his hand tightened around her shoulder. 'Remember what I once said about sparks?' he asked.

'Yes,' she whispered.

'The sparks are still there, Jessica. One day we will go to bed together.'

'You don't know that.' Her voice was a little unsteady.

'Not now—the children will be waking soon. But one day. I'm sure of it, Jessica.'

CHAPTER SIX

'You won't be needing that today.'

Jessica looked up as tanned fingers whisked the paint brush out of her hand. 'I won't?'

Dark eyes sparkled down at her. 'We're going out for the day.'

'But the children have just gone off to school. They won't be back for a few hours, Kirk.'

'Betty has undertaken to look after them when they do get back.'

'We could wait...'

He touched her hair, pushing back a strand that had fallen forward over her forehead. 'You don't understand, Jessica. This day is just for us. No children. No responsibilities. No remembering that we're an aunt and an uncle. Just you and me, enjoying ourselves.'

Her senses leaped as she looked into the laughing face. Not a sign of the vulnerability she had seen on that night a few days earlier. Kirk was his usual sensuous, macho self today—attractive, strong, sexy beyond compare.

'Do you know how to ride, Jessica?'

'I wish I did.'

'Game to give it a try?'

'I'd love to!'

She did not know the picture she made, with her green eyes shining, her lips curved in an eager smile and her fair hair tumbling loosely over her shoulders. Kirk's gaze lingered on her face a few seconds and a tiny muscle moved in his jaw. As he moved towards her, she held her breath.

But then he straightened. 'You know I want to kiss you. But if I do, we'll never get away.' With what looked like a conscious effort he stepped away from her. 'Have to get you fitted out,' he said briskly.

Bemused, wishing he had not been so strong-minded about not kissing her, Jessica watched him leave the room. A few minutes later he was back and handing her a pair of khaki riding-breeches.

'Linda's?' she asked, startled.

'Not Linda's,' he said, very gently, as if he understood the emotions Jessica would have felt at wearing clothes that had so recently belonged to her sister. 'These belonged to my mother. She was about the same size as you.'

The breeches were an almost perfect fit. Fifteen minutes later, Jessica was watching as Kirk saddled the horses—Thunder, a tall black horse, for himself, and Nan, a smaller light brown mare, for Jessica.

'She's gentle,' Kirk told her, as he helped her to mount. 'Ideal for a first-time ride.'

He showed her how to hold the reins and how to position her feet in the stirrups. His hands were on her hands, guiding her, and then on her legs. Jessica, who knew very well that he would be behaving no differently with anyone else who was learning to ride, had to steel herself not to reveal how affected she was by his touch.

After a practice walk around the stable yard, so that she could get used to the feel of the horse, Kirk mounted his own steed. He motioned to Jessica to follow him through the gate. Side by side, the horses began to walk along the sandy farm road.

'Comfortable?' Kirk asked after a few minutes.

She turned her head and smiled at him. 'Very.'

'Ready to try a trot?'

'What do I have to do?'

There was a smile in his eyes as he instructed her. A minute later they were both trotting, Thunder a little ahead of Nan now.

And then Kirk slowed his horse and waited for Nan to come up alongside. 'How does it feel, Jessica?'

'*Wonderful!* I don't know why I didn't learn to ride long ago.'

'I'm glad you didn't. It's nice to think that I'm your first teacher,' he said, and just for a second there was an expression in his face that reminded her of the moment when he'd been about to kiss her.

He let Thunder trot once more and the horse gained some ground again. Watching the easy movement of the broad shoulders in front of her, Jessica thought what a dynamic man Kirk was. The virile body, the laughter in his eyes, the things he said—how could any woman not feel special in his company? Just for a moment she found herself thinking of Alicia.

Then Kirk turned his horse off the road and on to a path that led through the vineyards, and all thoughts of Alicia went out of Jessica's head.

It was a beautiful day. The sun warmed her face and arms. Insects buzzed in the vineyards, and the air was sweet from a bit of rain that had fallen, a little unexpectedly, the previous night. In the distance the mountains, so often translucent, were clearly defined against the cloudless sky.

Where the path was wide enough for two horses, they rode alongside each other. Otherwise Kirk rode in front, turning his head now and then to see how Jessica was getting on.

Towards midday they stopped. They had been riding steadily in the direction of the mountains, and now they were on the first high slope of land. Kirk vaulted to the ground. Putting his hands on Jessica's waist, he helped her down too.

'Enjoying yourself?' he asked.

'Loving every moment.'

His hands were still on her waist, and he was standing so close to her that when she looked up at his face she saw golden lights in his eyes.

'You're a spunky woman, Jessica.'

She danced him a smile. 'I should hope so!'

'I should have warned you—your legs may hurt a bit tomorrow.'

'I don't care if they do. This is all so perfect, it's worth a little pain.'

The laughter lines around his eyes deepened. 'Time for a break.'

He led the horses to a nearby stream. When he came back to Jessica he was carrying two cartons of fruit juice, a few biscuits and some apples, all of which he had stored in a saddlebag.

A little way downstream from where the horses drank, Jessica and Kirk sat down with their lunch. Around them the long grasses hissed and rippled in the breeze. A few *dassies*, little grey rock-rabbits, played on the sun-warmed stone, and overhead a widow-bird dragged its long black tail cumbersomely through the air.

'It's so peaceful here,' Jessica said after a while.

'We don't have to go any further if you don't want to.'

'What did you have planned?'

'There's a view I wanted to show you.'

'In that case, I want to see it. I wish I'd brought a camera, Kirk.'

He smiled at her. 'Next time.'

Next time. Funny how two simple words could sound so beautiful. Jessica lay back against a rock, enjoying the heat of it through her clothes, and wishing there was a way she could make the day last for ever.

They went on after a while. On horseback once more, Jessica felt a stiffening in her thighs, but she decided not to mention it.

They were quite high up and near the edge of a mountain ridge when Kirk motioned her to rein in her horse. Jessica was astonished when he told her to dismount—even more astonished when he lifted her on to his own horse.

'What on earth——?' she asked, when she was seated behind him on Thunder's saddle. Kirk was holding both sets of reins now, and Nan, gentle horse that she was, followed obediently behind Thunder.

'I told you there's a view I want you to see. But there's not much of a path from here, and what there is is pretty steep going.'

'You don't think I could handle it?'

'People have been known to get dizzy up here. Hold on to me, Jessica.'

Jessica would not have got dizzy. She had always had a good head for heights, and, novice horsewoman though she was, she nevertheless believed she would have been up to the ride. But she put her arms round Kirk's waist and thrilled to the closeness with the man she loved more and more all the time.

As the horses began to move, she closed her eyes. She was tingling with an intense excitement as she felt the long male body against her own, the curve of Kirk's back against her chest, his thighs and calves against hers. His body moved with the swaying of the horse, and her own body moved with them both. Her heart beat so hard and so fast that she wondered if Kirk could feel it.

She only opened her eyes when the horses stopped and she heard Kirk say, 'Quite a view, Jessica?'

'Quite a view,' she agreed unsteadily.

In fact, it was a few seconds before her eyes would focus properly on the view. When they did, she understood why Kirk had brought her here. Spread out beneath them were valleys of vineyards in a spectacular tapestry of green and brown and purple. Surrounding the valleys, guarding them, were the mountains. It was one of the loveliest sights Jessica had ever seen.

'We'll come up here again,' said Kirk. He had turned his head now and was looking at her. 'And we'll make sure not to forget your camera.'

'I'd like that very much.'

'Think you could have managed the ride on your own?' There was an enigmatic expression in his face, almost as if he knew something of the emotional turmoil he had put her through.

'Perhaps.' She made herself smile as she met his eyes. 'I'm sure I can manage the way down alone.'

His eyes held hers for so long that Jessica had to fight a sudden wild trembling.

'The first bit's tricky,' he said, just when she was certain she could not hold that gaze a second longer. 'I'll let you go back on Nan as soon as it's safe.'

Expertly he turned the horses on a piece of ground that was so narrow that one false step could have sent riders and horses hurtling down the cliffside. It would have been so easy for Jessica to let herself lean against him once more as they started down the rocky track. But this time she kept herself deliberately apart from him. Of necessity her hands had to be on his waist—if she did not hold on to him she would fall—but she kept her head high and her eyes firmly open. The instant the path widened, she insisted on mounting Nan.

The ride up the mountain had been one of the most exciting experiences of her life—definitely the most erotic. It had also shaken her to the very depths of her being. For the sake of her sanity, she was not ready yet to repeat the experience.

In the late afternoon they came to a tavern. It was a lonely place, well off the beaten track and known only to a few cherished regulars. Kirk knew the proprietor, Jan, a huge, bearded man who welcomed him with a

NO COST! NO OBLIGATION TO BUY! NO PURCHASE NECESSARY!

PLAY "LUCKY 7" AND GET AS MANY AS SIX FREE GIFTS...

HOW TO PLAY:

1. With a coin, carefully scratch off the silver box opposite. You will now be eligible to receive one or more free books, and possibly other gifts, depending on what is revealed beneath the scratch off area.

2. When you return this card, you'll receive specially selected Mills & Boon Romances. We'll send you the books and gifts you qualify for **absolutely free**, and at the same time we'll reserve you a subscription to our Reader Service.

3. If we don't hear from you, we'll then send you six brand new Romances to read and enjoy every month for just £1.60 each, the same price as the books in the shops. There is no extra charge for postage and handling. There are no hidden extras.

4. When you join the Mills & Boon Reader Service, you'll also get our free monthly Newsletter; featuring author news, horoscopes, penfriends and competitions.

5. You are under no obligation, and may cancel or suspend your subscription at any time simply by writing to us.

You'll love your
cuddly teddy.
His brown eyes and
cute face are sure to
make you smile.

PLAY "LUCKY 7"

Just scratch off the silver box with a coin.
Then check below to see which gifts you get.

YES! I have scratched off the silver box. Please send me all
the gifts for which I qualify. I understand I am under no
obligation to purchase any books, as explained on the opposite
page. I am over 18 years of age.

MS/MRS/MISS/MR _____ 2A2R

ADDRESS _____

_____

_____

POSTCODE _____ SIGNATURE _____

7	7	7	WORTH FOUR FREE BOOKS, FREE TEDDY BEAR AND MYSTERY GIFT
🍒	🍒	🍒	WORTH FOUR FREE BOOKS AND MYSTERY GIFT
●	●	●	WORTH FOUR FREE BOOKS
🔔	🔔	🍒	WORTH TWO FREE BOOKS

-1-

Mills & Boon Reader Service
Freepost
P.O. Box 236
Croydon
Surrey
CR9 9EL

No
Stamp
Needed

shout and a bear-hug. For Jessica there was a quieter greeting, as well as a curious look, almost as if Jan was more used to seeing Kirk with someone else.

Kirk tethered the horses to an old-fashioned hitching post, then they followed Jan to a table on a stone-floored veranda that was covered with pale yellow jasmine and scarlet bougainvillaea, and sat and looked out over a vista of vineyards.

'Will you trust me to order?' Kirk asked, when Jan had left them alone to examine the menu. 'The selection might be sparse, but everything is delicious.'

'I trust you,' she said, knowing she would trust him with far more serious things than the ordering of a meal. Life itself, maybe.

'How about some *bredie* with salad and Jan's special home-made bread?'

'Sounds delicious.'

The food looked delicious too when Jan brought it to their table—plump pieces of mutton, stewed with tomatoes and onions and spiced with peppercorns, a tossed green salad and the grainiest bread Jessica had ever seen. And, accompanying the meal, a bottle of red wine.

'I don't suppose I need ask whether the wine was made in these valleys?' Jessica shot Kirk a smile when Jan had walked away from their table.

'Anything else would be heresy, wouldn't it?'

When Kirk had poured the wine he said, 'What shall we drink to, Jessica? More outings like today?'

'Like today,' she said lightly, and wondered if he could see her happiness in her eyes as they clinked glasses.

'You've enjoyed the day, Jessica?'

Her eyes met his. 'You know the answer to that, Kirk.'

'I get the feeling that you're a person who's not afraid of life, Jessica. That you plunge right in, and have a good time wherever you are.'

'I never thought about it before, but I suppose that's true.'

'I like a woman who's fun and eager and passionate.' His eyes were on her lips now.

'I may be eager and fun, but you don't know a darned thing about my passions,' she said, over the thudding in her ears.

'They're there, Jessica, burning under all that surface innocence.'

'You talk as if you know me, Kirk, but you don't. Just because Linda was my twin it doesn't mean you know me.'

'Actually, apart from your appearance you're not at all like Linda.'

'Kirk . . . don't!'

'And besides, you're wrong. I do know you. There are things I know without actually knowing them.'

Across the table, he reached for her hand. There was nothing playful in the way he held it.

'Have there been other men, Jessica?' he asked softly.

She sucked in her breath. 'That shouldn't concern you.'

'I want to know. You're so beautiful, I'd find it hard to believe there's been nobody.'

'I have gone out with different men.'

'Anyone serious?'

'Not really.'

'Not really?'

'All right, then—no.'

'Why not?'

'It's just the way it's been.' Her voice shook. She could hardly tell him that she had never forgotten their first encounter; that, though she had tried not to think of him in the six and a half years that had passed, he had always been there somehow in her mind, spoiling her for other men even when she had not been conscious of the fact.

'Are you saying you've never been in love?'

'I've loved a man.' It was an effort to keep her voice steady.

His face was sombre. 'And he?'

She shrugged.

'Was there someone else?'

Jessica thought of Alicia—beautiful Alicia. A man would have to be blind not to be attracted to her. Linda had said it was only a matter of time before she and Kirk were married.

'I think so,' she said painfully.

'Jessica...'

She withdrew her hand from his. 'Do you mind?' she said, 'I'd really rather not go on talking about it.'

'All right,' he said. She did not notice that his eyes had turned a little bleak.

They barely talked as they rode back home. It was as if they both had things on their minds.

It was almost dark as they rode up the long farm road. Donny and Laura must have heard them coming, for they ran into the stable yard just as Jessica was getting off her horse.

Suddenly all was noisy chatter. Donny wanted to know where they had been and why they had not waited for him to go along. Laura had made a new friend at nursery school and asked if she could invite her to Bergview. Leaving Kirk to tend to the horses, Jessica left the stable yard with the children. She was very quiet, but Donny and Laura did not seem to notice it; they both talked all the way back to the house.

After supper Jessica helped Laura with her bath, while Kirk listened to Donny's grade one reading homework. Neither child wanted to go to bed. Tomorrow was Saturday—no school—and so please, please, please could they stay up late, just this once?

Jessica and Kirk did not exchange another private word for the rest of the evening.

Much later, when the children were in bed at last and Jessica had gone to her room and changed into her pyjamas, there was a knock at her door.

'Kirk,' she said, without surprise, as she opened the door.

'Did you think those kids would *ever* get to bed?'

'They were certainly lively tonight, weren't they? Still, it's good to see them looking so much happier.'

'Are you going to keep me talking at the door, or may I come in, Jessica?'

She hesitated. 'It's very late...'

'You're scared to let me in?' His eyes had narrowed.

She was scared of *herself*. Wondering just how far she could trust herself if she did let him in. But she managed to look at him calmly. 'The children might wonder...'

'Asleep, both of them. And your legs must be starting to hurt.'

'A little,' she admitted.

'I've brought you some ointment. You're not really going to go prim on me and keep me standing out here in the passage, Jessica?' His eyes glittered.

Kirk was right—she *had* gone prim on him. He could not know that she was feeling tense about an intimacy which she longed for and yet simultaneously feared because it meant so much to her.

'Well, are you going to let me in?' he drawled.

'Why not?' she said brightly, and stepped aside for him.

Kirk closed the door and looked at her. 'Your legs might be sore by tomorrow. Let me see them.'

They were sore already. 'Why don't you just give me the ointment, Kirk?' she said.

'I want to see for myself how much damage there is. You might need something different.'

'I'm not a child, Kirk. I can take care of myself.'

'I know you can.' His eyes were moving over her body in a way that unnerved her. 'And you're right—you're not a child. You're a woman—a very beautiful woman.'

'Give me the ointment.' Her voice was unsteady.

'Not before you show me your legs.'

A quiver went through Jessica as she looked at him. She did not want to show him her legs, but she knew he would not go until she did. Slowly, she sat down on the bed and pushed up her pyjamas.

Kirk knelt by her side. With that rare gentleness she had glimpsed in him sometimes, he parted her knees and touched the raw skin of her inner thighs.

'*Jessica!*' There was intense remorse in his voice.

'It's all right, Kirk, really it is. It isn't as bad as it looks.'

'We should have turned back after we had our lunch.'

'Nonsense,' she said. 'I had a wonderful day. Don't you remember me saying it was worth a bit of pain?'

'Not as much as this. I should have known your skin would be soft... I'm going to put the ointment on for you, Jessica.'

'I can do it myself,' she protested.

'I won't be satisfied unless I know it's been applied properly.'

'*Come on*, Kirk!'

'On second thoughts,' he said, 'maybe you should have a bath first.'

'You're not going to tell me you need to help me with that as well,' she said drily.

'Now that *is* a thought!'

'I was joking,' she said hastily.

'But I wasn't.' His eyes were sparkling with the devilment she was beginning to know so well. 'There's nothing I'd like better than to take a bath with you, Jessica.'

It shocked her to realise how much they both wanted the same thing.

'One day we will bath together,' he said.

She summoned her firmest voice. 'I think you'd better go now, Kirk.'

'When you've had your bath and your ointment.'

'This is ridiculous!'

'If you insist,' he said, 'I'll wait in this room while you bath.'

'I absolutely do insist.'

'As long as you understand that I insist on putting on the ointment for you myself afterwards.'

Closing the bathroom door firmly behind her, Jessica ran the water and threw in some scented bath salts. When the tub was almost full she climbed in and lay down in the water to soak.

She remained in the water much longer than she had to, letting in more warm water when it turned cold. But the moment came when she had to get out. She towelled herself dry, then ran a brush through her damp hair and applied some perfume to her wrists and behind her ears. On an impulse, she dabbed a bit between her breasts as well.

Kirk might call her a tease—and he would be absolutely right—but for the first time in her life she was so much in love that nothing else seemed to matter.

He was standing at the window. He turned as she came out of the bathroom, and for a long moment he stood motionless, just looking at her. Then he walked towards her.

'You've got the ointment?' she asked, a little jerkily.

'The ointment? Oh, yes, the ointment...' Something moved in his throat.

'Well, then...if you really want to... Although I'm sure I can put it on myself.'

'I told you I was going to do it,' he said softly. 'Sit down, Jessica.'

There was no chair in the room. Jessica was trembling a little as she sat down on the bed. Once more Kirk knelt on the floor by her feet, then he began to apply the ointment.

If there was any pain, Jessica did not feel it. Her eyes were on Kirk's hands—big, hard hands which had no trouble performing tasks which required the utmost in physical strength. Today she had seen those hands on the reins of a strong-willed horse; for a time they had even controlled two sets of reins. Now there was only gentleness in those hands, and it was a gentleness which made her throat thick with emotion.

'There,' he said at length.

'Thank you,' she whispered.

'Do you think you'll be all right now, Jessica?'

'I know I will be.'

'Good.'

'You can go now, Kirk.'

He was still kneeling, but his body had straightened, and his eyes were on a level with her breasts. 'I want to stay,' he said.

'Kirk...'

She tried to stand up, but in that moment he put his arms round her waist and drew her against him.

'The children...' she said weakly.

'Both sleeping, you know that. And I've locked the door.'

'You think of everything,' she said shakily.

'Maybe that's because I've thought of little else lately.' He drew himself further up, so that he could rub his cheeks against her face.

'I warned you what to expect when you first came here, Jessica. You're so beautiful, so sexy and desirable. All I want to do is make love to you.'

She looked at him mutely, wanting him more than she had known she could want a man, yet unable to answer him.

'And today I thought you wanted it too, Jessica. On the mountain, when you were sitting behind me on

Thunder's saddle. I had a feeling that if I'd kissed you you wouldn't have minded.'

'Kirk . . .'

'Was I right, Jessica?'

'You were right,' she whispered.

He leaned back so that he could look at her. And then he cupped her face in his hands, drew it towards him and began to kiss her. She gave a start as he caught her upper lip between his so that she could feel his teeth. But as the sheer delight of what was happening overcame her, she relaxed against him with a shudder. He did not have to coax her to open her mouth; she knew it was what he wanted, but it was what she wanted too, and she parted her lips willingly.

A sob of pleasure rose in her throat as he began to kiss her more and more passionately, his tongue exploring the sweetness of her mouth, claiming, seeking, demanding a response from her. She gave him all the response he could have asked for. She had never made love with a man, but there was an abandon in her now as she kissed him too, a rising tide of female feelings that she had never known existed: primitive, primeval, buried deep inside her until this moment.

She did not resist when Kirk pushed her backwards on the bed. When he half covered her body with his, her arms went round him. There was no thought now, no nervousness of the point that was fast approaching. She quivered with her need for him, a need that was as strong as the one signalled by the throbbing strength of his own body.

Unbuttoning her pyjama top, he drew it off her shoulders. And then his hands were on her breasts, caressing them until the nipples darkened and hardened. When he began to kiss her breasts, his lips going where his fingers had been, her hands moved over his back, revelling in the touch and shape of him, clutching feverishly at his shoulders.

She was only momentarily startled when he began to push down her pyjama pants. Caught in the grip of an emotion that was like nothing she had ever experienced, she made no move to stop him. She craved fulfilment as much as Kirk did.

And then suddenly she remembered that there were things she had to tell him. Things she had forgotten in the raw emotions of the moment.

She was about to speak, when there was the sound of the door handle moving.

They both froze. The handle moved again. Frantic with panic, Jessica tried to push away from Kirk.

He put his hand over her mouth. 'The door's locked,' he reminded her very quietly.

Once more the handle moved. Then Laura's voice came through the door. 'Aunty Jess!'

For a moment Jessica was unable to answer, but Kirk nodded to her, and she managed to call, 'Yes?'

'I can't open the door, Aunty Jess.'

'Speak naturally,' Kirk whispered.

'What is it, honey?' Jessica called.

'My throat hurts. Open the door, Aunty Jess!'

'I'm coming, honey...'

'Please open the door!'

'Go to your room, Laura,' Jessica called. 'I'll be with you in a minute.'

'But, Aunty Jess——'

'Go to bed, Laura. I'm coming.'

'OK...' said an unhappy voice, after which there was silence.

Jessica waited half a minute to make sure that Laura had indeed moved away from the door. 'I have to go to her,' she said then.

'Yes, I know. I'll be waiting for you when you get back, Jessica.'

'No.' She shook her head.

The warm, hard body had rolled away from hers. Kirk looked at her. 'Jessica!'

'Please, Kirk. When you're certain I'm in Laura's room and that she isn't wandering around the house, go to your own room.'

'We started something tonight.'

'I know we did. But it was obviously never meant to be.'

'You don't know what you're saying.'

'I do,' she said flatly. 'I'll see you in the morning.'

Laura was sitting up in bed when Jessica came into the room.

'Why did you lock the door, Aunty Jess?'

'It's something I do sometimes,' Jessica said briskly. 'Tell me about your throat, Laura.'

'It hurts.'

Jessica put her hand on Laura's forehead and then on her chest. The little girl didn't seem to have a fever, for the skin was cool to the touch.

'I'm going to make you some warm lemon juice with a bit of honey and lots of sugar,' Jessica said. 'I'm sure that will make you feel better.'

'Mommy made that too when my throat hurt.'

'Maybe that's because your grandmother made it for us when we were your age.' Jessica smiled down at the little girl. 'And if your throat's still sore in the morning we'll go and see the doctor.'

'OK...'

In the kitchen, Jessica squeezed a lemon into a glass of warm water, then sweetened it as she had promised. All the while she was thinking of Kirk, and of what had so nearly happened between them. Her body, denied the fulfilment it longed for, ached with frustration. It was not difficult to guess how Kirk, alone in his own bed once more, must be feeling.

Back in Laura's room, she gave the little girl her drink. Laura sipped it very slowly, and by the time the glass was empty she actually did seem more comfortable. Jessica pulled the blanket up over her shoulders, kissed her, said goodnight, and switched off the light.

She was amazed to find Kirk still in her room. A decorous Kirk now, dressed and standing at the window once more.

Jessica stared at him in astonishment. 'I didn't expect to find you here.'

'Did you really think I could just go back to my room after what happened between us?'

He came towards her, but as he tried to draw her close she stiffened.

'No, Kirk. No! Laura could come back—or Donny.'

'I know that. We won't make love, Jessica. At least not tonight.'

'You have to go.'

'We have to talk.'

'We can do that in the morning.'

'What I have to say can't wait.' Kirk took her hands in his. 'I want you to marry me, Jessica.'

She looked at him, utterly stunned. 'I don't understand...'

'I want you to be my wife. Soon.'

She began to tremble. 'Why? Why now...suddenly...?'

'You know how I feel about you, Jessica. You're so beautiful, so sexy. Tonight isn't the first time I've wanted to make love to you. I've been wanting it ever since you came to Bergview the first time.'

'Kirk...'

'What happened tonight...we can't have a repetition of that. One of the children looking for you, wondering why the door's locked. I want us to share a room. And I want to do it openly. What do you say, Jessica?'

'I . . . I don't know what to say.'

'It's easy, darling. Just say yes. You wanted me tonight too. You would have slept with me if Laura hadn't disturbed us.'

After she had told him she was a virgin, and made sure he was protected—yes, she would have slept with him, she knew that.

'I want you so badly, Jessica. I want to make love to you as often as possible—every night.' He pulled her against him and held her close. 'Will you marry me?'

So much talk about making love. *But not a single word about loving her.* More than anything in the world, Jessica wanted to say yes to him. But there was a vestige of pride left in her that demanded more, that had to know that he was not only after her body. *That needed to hear him say he loved her.*

'Will you, Jessica?'

'You'll have to give me time,' she said.

'How much time?'

'A few days . . .'

'A few days? Don't you know what you want?'

'I need time to think, Kirk,' she said. 'Just a few days, then I'll give you my answer.'

CHAPTER SEVEN

'DID you say you were leaving tomorrow, Alicia?'

'That's right.' Alicia turned her face to the sun, as if to soak up all the warmth she could. 'Think of me shivering in Europe while you two are basking in the sun here at Bergview!'

Kirk laughed. 'We'll do that, won't we, Jessica? How long will you be gone this time, Alicia?'

'Almost three weeks. Most of it in France, of course, but there may be a few other stops as well. Do you know, Kirk, I'd dearly love to go skiing in Switzerland again. Remember the wonderful time we had in San Moritz two years ago?'

'It was fun,' he acknowledged.

Alicia looked at Jessica. 'We stayed in this marvellous wooden chalet. It was the most gorgeous place you can imagine, all great big fireplaces and priceless antiques everywhere. And so cosy! After a long day on the slopes we'd curl up in front of the fireplace with hot spiced apples and mulled wine. And then there were times we didn't feel like going skiing at all...' She gave Kirk a private glance from beneath lowered lashes. 'Oh, it was wonderful!'

'Sounds like fun,' Jessica said, very lightly, and tried to ignore the pain in the pit of her stomach.

'Why don't we plan to do it again some time soon, darling?'

Alicia, her voice low and husky, was concentrating on Kirk once more. No stranger would have taken her for the efficient owner and manager of a huge wine estate. With her long shapely limbs revealed to best advantage

by her tiny bikini, she could have passed quite easily for
a model.

'What do you say, Kirk?'

He grinned. 'Some of us have work to do, Alicia.'

'Come on, darling!' she reproached. 'As if I didn't
know that. But the beauty of our situation has always
been that you and I work at the same thing. We go to
the same places, we know the same people. A few weeks
doing the nitty-gritty in Europe, then some time off to
play. Doesn't that sound good?' Her voice dropped to
a lower level. 'And we've always enjoyed playing at the
same things, haven't we, darling?'

'I don't think any of this can be of great interest to
Jessica,' he said mildly.

'Oh, I *am* sorry, Jessica, I didn't mean to bore you.
I only thought... Kirk, darling, really, I mean it, why
don't we give it some thought?'

Kirk shook his head. 'I'm not planning any trips at
this moment.'

'Well, think about it anyway.'

'The only thing I can think about right now is how
inviting that water looks. I'm going in for a swim.'

He stood at the edge of the pool a moment, his body
tanned and beautiful, then he dived into the water. When
he surfaced, he called to the children, 'Anyone want to
go in the water with me?'

'Me! Me!' they shouted together as they tore off the
shirts they wore over their swimsuits.

'Sun-tan oil first,' Jessica insisted, and they shifted
their feet impatiently on the slastoed edge of the pool,
while she rubbed oil over their warm bodies.

'You're really into this mothering bit, aren't you?'
Alicia remarked, when Donny and Laura had run off to
join Kirk in the water.

The contempt in her voice was deliberate, but Jessica
had decided not to let Alicia rattle her. 'I enjoy the
children,' was all she said.

Her eyes were on Kirk, who had climbed out of the pool in order to help Laura into the water. He looked so sexy that Jessica felt desire springing to life inside her.

A week had passed since Kirk had asked her to marry him, and she had not yet given him an answer. Much as she wanted to be his wife—and she wanted it more than anything in the world—thus far she had found it impossible to make a decision.

Not once since the evening in her room had they had any physical contact. Jessica wondered sometimes whether Kirk lay sleepless, as she did, aching for the fulfilment of making love. It was an ache that never left her. An ache that was intensified as she watched the almost naked body at the side of the pool. She was still no nearer a solution.

'Enjoying life at Bergview?' asked Alicia.

'It's very pleasant.'

'Pleasant!' The contempt had deepened. 'How boring! How old are you, Jessica? Twenty-four, twenty-five? Surely you want more than pleasantness in your life? Something more than sitting at home all day caring for some other woman's children.'

'My sister's children,' Jessica pointed out quietly.

'Your sister, OK. Nevertheless, you were independent, you earned your own living; how can you possibly be content with the life you lead now?'

'I'm still earning a living, Alicia. The calendar sketches are finished, and I've been given another assignment.'

'Freelance work.' Alicia's tone was dismissive. 'Isn't that an iffy kind of thing at best? Now you have it, now you don't. Don't you *miss* what you had before? The people, the excitement?'

'Not really,' Jessica said, wondering how Alicia could be quite so nosy and insensitive.

'What about men? Didn't you leave behind a man in Johannesburg?'

'Nobody serious.'

Alicia had been watching Kirk, playing in the water with the children. At the last words she swung round. Her face was hard, her eyes assessing. 'Have you fallen for Kirk?'

A flush appeared in Jessica's cheeks. 'Do you always pry like this?'

'So you *have* fallen for him! Don't you realise you're not his type? Kirk's used to worldly, sophisticated women. He and Tom never had the same taste in females.'

'Look, can we talk about something else? This trip you're going on, Alicia. Will you——'

'Next thing you'll be telling me you're expecting to marry him!'

Jessica's flush deepened.

'You haven't discussed marriage, have you, Jessica? *Have you?*'

Jessica did not answer.

Alicia was staring very hard at her now, her face red and angry. 'Damn you, Jessica, why don't you answer me?'

Jessica glanced at the pool. Her conversation with Alicia would not be heard above the noisy splashing.

'All right,' she said quietly, 'if you must know, Kirk has asked me to marry him.'

Alicia sat upright in her chaise-longue. Her face was pale suddenly, her expression even tighter and harder than before. 'Does that mean you're engaged? Kirk hasn't said anything.'

'That's because I haven't given him an answer yet.'

'What will the answer be? Are you going to marry him?'

'This really isn't any of your business, Alicia. I only told you about it at all because you were so insistent.' Jessica was starting to feel very angry.

'*Are you going to marry him?*'

'I don't know.'

Alicia pushed her hand through her perfectly groomed hair. Suddenly she laughed, a short, sharp laugh. 'Clever, clever Kirk! Oh, but you have to hand it to the man. Securing a mother for his brother's children so that he won't have to take the responsibility for them himself. Because that's all it is, you know.'

'Stop this, Alicia!'

'A mother who's the image of the one they used to have. I told you once before that was all he was after. He must have been desperate when he proposed to you. Must have imagined you'd tire of the quiet farm life sooner or later, and then where would he be? Clever man!'

'I don't want to listen to this, Alicia.'

'Why not? After all, I'm not the only one you'll hear it from, Jessica. A mother for the children and a passably pretty woman for his bed. Wonderful!'

Jessica sat through this speech feeling numb. That Alicia was being spiteful was clear. Unfortunately, what she was saying coincided with the things Jessica had been thinking ever since Kirk's unexpected proposal.

'Still, I have to give you credit for being cautious,' Alicia went on. 'I'd put you down as the kind of ninny who'd jump at the chance of marrying a rich man—as Linda did. Obviously your career means more to you than I realised. And who'd want to be a substitute mother anyway?'

Much more of this and Jessica would lose her temper and say something she would later regret. Far better to remove herself from Alicia's company. She stood up, said there was something she had to do indoors, and was about to walk away when Alicia gripped her arm.

'Did you know, Jessica, that before the boating accident Kirk and I had been discussing marriage?'

'Linda said something...'

'So your sister talked about me. I thought she might have. Well, no wonder, she used to see us together all the time. She didn't seem to like me very much. I made her feel insecure in some way, I suppose. Did she tell you that Kirk and I go back a long time?'

'She mentioned you were friends.'

'More than just friends. Well, then, you know how things stand. It's a relationship that won't change, Jessica. Whether Kirk marries someone else or not, we'll always go on seeing each other.'

'If you were in fact discussing marriage, why did you stop?' Jessica made herself ask the question.

'As I said, there was the accident. And then you arrived on the scene, with all your obvious advantages.' Alicia shrugged. 'I'm not Linda's twin sister. I don't look like her. I'm not like her in any way. I can't take Linda's place with the children in quite the same way you can— at least, not in Kirk's eyes. And darling Kirk seems to have developed an unjustified sense of responsibility.'

'Are you always so vicious, Alicia?'

'Vicious?' Alicia gave a short hard laugh. 'I'm just stating facts, Jessica.'

'Are you in love with Kirk?' Another question Jessica forced herself to ask. But she had to know the answer.

'Love?' Alicia shrugged. 'Kirk is an extremely attractive man and a very rich one. We get on well together—we always did. We work well together too. A merger between our two estates would be perfect.'

'You're talking business, not love.'

'Not only business.' Alicia shot her a nasty look. 'Kirk is pretty fantastic in bed. But you already know that, don't you, Jessica?'

Jessica was beginning to feel a little ill, but having gone this far she had to go on. 'If I didn't marry Kirk...if you were to get engaged to him after all...how would you feel about the children?'

'They need a bit of mothering at the moment, I can see that. But between Betty and myself, we would manage.'

'And you wouldn't mind being a mother for Donny and Laura?'

'Why not, when the bigger package is so attractive? Besides which, I wouldn't be bothered with the kids for more than a couple of years.'

'I don't understand.'

'It won't be long before they're ready to go to boarding-school.'

'*Boarding-school!* Donny's six years old, for heaven's sake! Laura isn't even five. You can't seriously be thinking about boarding-school already, Alicia?'

'Whyever not? People send their kids to school all the time. Seven isn't too young to go away. Good heavens, Jessica, don't look at me like that! I'm not some monster. I'm a contemporary woman, a career woman. I enjoy going to parties, I adore travelling. You don't really imagine I'd tolerate having a pair of snotty-nosed kids tying me to my home forever?'

'Linda would never have allowed her children to be sent away.'

'I don't mean to sound callous, Jessica, but your sister's no longer around to make decisions.'

'Kirk wouldn't stand for it either. He loves Donny and Laura. He wants the best for them, and it's important to him that they remain at Bergview.'

'Grow up, Jessica. Granted, Kirk is being boringly conscientious about his responsibilities right now. It's what I said a few minutes ago. Thank heaven, that won't last. Kirk won't want the kids around for ever either.'

'I don't believe you.'

'Trust me.' Alicia smiled her odious smile. 'I know Kirk better than you do. We've always been two of a kind, Kirk and I. That's why we get on so well.'

'I will never let either of you send Linda's children away!' Jessica's face was pale now, her voice fierce.

'If I were mistress of Bergview there wouldn't be a thing you could do to stop me.'

'You're wrong,' Jessica said grimly. 'There's nothing—
absolutely nothing, Alicia—I wouldn't do to prevent
those children from being chased out of their home.'

Alicia said she still had some packing to do that evening,
so they had an early *braaivleis* by the pool. Betty had
prepared a big platter of steak and *boerewors*, and Jessica
had made a few salads. Kirk saw to the fire and the meat.

The children took their plates to a nearby hammock,
leaving the adults to eat alone. Mainly, the talking was
done by Kirk and Alicia. Alicia began to discuss a play
she and Kirk had seen together in Cape Town some
months earlier. Jessica had seen the play too, before
coming to Bergview, and she could have joined in the
conversation. But she was unable to focus on fictional
characters when the real characters who peopled her life
were in crisis.

'You're very quiet, Jessica,' Kirk remarked once.
'Something bothering you?'

'Nothing at all.' She managed a light smile, and he
seemed content with that, for he turned his attention
back to Alicia.

The talk changed to wine-related matters—grapes and
wine estates and the state of world prices. Animated
discussion about a topic of which Jessica had little
knowledge, and now Kirk and Alicia seemed not to notice
how quiet she had become.

Presently Alicia looked at her watch and said it was
time to go. Jessica waited till the Porsche was out of
sight, then she turned to Kirk.

'We need to talk.'

An alert look appeared in the eyes that met hers. His
glance swept her face, as if in a question.

'I thought there was something on your mind,' he said.

'Yes. Kirk, I——'

'Later,' he said quietly. 'When the children are asleep.'

Almost as if they knew the turmoil Jessica was in, Donny and Laura did everything they could to avoid going to bed. Donny remembered several things that absolutely had to be done before he could get beneath the blankets. Laura insisted on three stories instead of one. At last, however, the lights in both rooms had been switched off.

From the living-room came the sound of music. Jessica stood in the darkened passage and tried to control breathing that was suddenly a little too fast. Now that the moment had come, she was nervous. Kirk had never repeated his proposal. What if he had changed his mind about marriage?

Her hand was on the door, about to open it, when she turned and went to her room. Quickly discarding her jeans, she changed into a turquoise linen dress with a soft flared skirt and a tight wide belt. In the mirror her eyes were a little too bright. In her throat her pulse ran to a crazy beat. She dashed cold water over her face, then sat down on her bed and took a few long calming breaths.

'Jessica,' said Kirk, when she entered the living-room.

The glance that took in her appearance was wholly male, lingering on the high swell of her breasts, on the tiny waist beneath the wide belt, sweeping down her bare legs to dainty open-toed sandals, it told her that he liked the way she looked. It also made her feel a little more confident.

'We need to talk,' she said again.

'We will,' he said softly. 'But first I want to dance with you.'

She took a step back. 'Afterwards. When we've had a chance to——'

'First,' he insisted, and, closing the distance between them, he took her in his arms.

The music was soft and he had turned the lights down low, as if he had planned for this moment. Holding her against him, his lips in her hair, he guided her slowly around the room, so slowly that it felt as if they were barely moving. And yet, with the long hard body so close against hers, every movement caused the blood to burn more fiercely in Jessica's veins.

'I've missed you,' he said, still with his lips in her hair.

'I haven't been away,' she whispered against his throat.

'It felt as if you were. A whole week without touching you once. Do you know what that does to a man, Jessica?'

'Tell me,' she murmured provocatively.

'I've ached to take you in my arms, to kiss you, to make love to you.'

'Why didn't you?'

'Witch,' he said. 'Beautiful, sexy little witch. You know only too well why I kept away.'

As he drew her closer still, Jessica curled one arm round his neck, the other round his waist. They went on dancing in silence until the music ended.

'Kirk...' she said then.

He held her a little away from him so that he could look down at her.

'All right, Jessica, let's talk.'

'Maybe... maybe we should sit down?'

His eyes were dark and enigmatic in the soft light, impossible to read. After a moment he loosened his hold on her and beckoned her to sit beside him on a velvet two-seater.

'Well, Jessica?'

'The other day... You asked me to marry you.'

'Exactly a week ago. I've been waiting for an answer ever since.'

Jessica swallowed on a throat that was suddenly dry. 'I'd like to be your wife, Kirk.'

'*Jessica!* My lovely Jessica! I've been hoping you'd say yes.'

'And now I have.'

'A whole week! I couldn't understand why it was taking you so long to make up your mind. I didn't know what to make of it.'

He pulled her against him and kissed her, so deeply, so passionately, that she felt dizzy.

At length he lifted his head. 'Our engagement calls for a bottle of the very best Bergview champagne. And I happen to have one cool and ready for the occasion.'

As he left the room, Jessica closed her eyes and leaned back against the soft velvet. A part of her was wildly excited at the thought of marrying Kirk; another part felt as confused as ever.

As much as she loved Kirk—and she loved him more than she had ever believed she could love anyone—it went against the grain to marry a man who had never once said he loved her. But she had made her sister a promise. And Alicia's malicious intentions towards the children left her with no other choice.

Kirk reappeared with glasses and champagne and they sat close together while they drank to their future.

'Let's set a date, Jessica,' said Kirk. 'I hate the way we're living now—separate bedrooms, terrified that the kids will appear if we do decide to make love. Would you mind if we made it very soon?'

'I'd like that too...'

'Next weekend?'

She laughed. 'That soon?'

'I'd make it even sooner if I thought it could be arranged.'

Jessica thought of Alicia, who would be away from the valley for a while. 'The weekend will be wonderful,' she agreed.

'You do realise it doesn't give us time to organise a big wedding?'

'Even if we did have the time, it would have to be a quiet affair,' she said soberly. 'Linda and Tommy... The accident is so recent that we couldn't have dancing and music.'

'Not unless we waited a few months,' he agreed. 'And I don't want to wait for you, Jessica.'

'I don't want that either,' she said with a rush of feeling.

And once more she thought of Alicia.

Laura was elated by the news of the wedding. 'Now you'll stay with us forever!' she shouted in glee.

Donny was outwardly more restrained. 'I'm glad, Aunty Jess,' he said. But he put his arms around her legs and hid his face against her skirt.

Betty was almost as excited as the children. 'I was so worried that Miss Alicia would be the new mistress,' she confessed when she was alone with Jessica. Then she asked whether she could bake the wedding cake.

Jessica's parents were still excavating in Italy, but for once she was able to contact them.

'This *is* a surprise!' her mother exclaimed, when she heard about the wedding.

'I knew it would be.'

'How wonderful for the children! I've been so concerned about them, Jess. If you hadn't been at Bergview to take care of them, I would have been there myself by now.'

Jessica laughed again. 'You're far happier grubbing about in the dirt for antiquities. Admit it, Mom.'

'Maybe I am. But I would have been there if my grandchildren had needed me.'

'Is there a chance you and Dad can make it back for the wedding, Mom?'

'We wouldn't miss it! I'll go into Rome the moment we finish talking and book our flights.' Her mother hesitated, then went on, 'Jess, darling, there is one thing I have to know... This wedding is so sudden. Forgive me, Jess, but are you doing this for the children?'

Jessica gripped the receiver tightly, a little shaken by her mother's unexpected perception. After a moment she said honestly, 'Partly...'

'Oh, Jess, that's no reason to get married. Close as you were to Linda, you don't have to do this.'

'I want to, Mom.'

'Do you love Kirk, Jessica?'

'I adore him,' Jessica said, without hesitation this time.

As she put down the receiver, it occurred to her that she had said to her mother what she had never been able to say to Kirk.

'Do you, Jessica, promise to love, cherish and honour this man?'

Jessica looked up at Kirk. 'I do,' she said, and her eyes were suddenly wet.

In that moment it did not matter why she had decided to marry him. All that mattered was that she would never love anyone as she loved him.

She looked at him again when the minister said, 'I now pronounce you man and wife.' Kirk was looking at her too, so tenderly that Jessica trembled. His hands went to her face, holding it beneath the veil, and her arms went up round his neck. For a few moments, as they kissed, she forgot that they were not alone.

Then a small voice said, 'Aunty Jess,' and she broke away from Kirk and bent to kiss the children: Laura, lovely in a pink and white chiffon dress; Donny, a little self-conscious in a suit his grandmother had bought for him.

Jessica kissed her father, who said gruffly, 'Congratulations, pet.' And then her mother whispered,

'Be happy, darling.' The eyes of both her parents were wet, and Jessica knew that in this moment of happiness they were also thinking of Linda and Tom. She swallowed hard to gulp back her own tears as the rest of the guests began to crowd around with their good wishes.

They had decided to hold the wedding on the lawns at Bergview. Contingency plans had been made to move the ceremony and the party indoors if the weather was bad, but the sun shone and the garden looked beautiful.

A smallish group stood around with champagne glasses in their hands. On Jessica's side there were only her parents, tanned and fit after months in the sun, yet looking a little older and very much sadder than when she had seen them last. Kirk had no parents, but two of his aunts and some cousins had been able to attend. He had invited all his closest friends as well—wine farmers from neighbouring estates and a few of the people he had gone to university with and with whom he had always kept in touch.

Alicia's mother was there, well-groomed and elegant in a grey silk suit. Jessica welcomed her with friendly words and a smile, but Mrs Mason kissed the air instead of Jessica's cheek, and her expression was frosty.

'Only Alicia's missing,' said Kirk. 'Jessica and I would have liked her to be here today as well.'

Mrs Mason's manner was no friendlier with Kirk. 'You could have delayed the wedding until Alicia's return.'

'We could have done that, but we didn't want to wait,' Kirk explained.

'I see.' Mrs Mason's lips tightened. Then, quite blatantly, she stared in the direction of Jessica's stomach.

Jessica was momentarily taken aback by the woman's outrageous behaviour, but then she regained her composure. Once she had decided to marry Kirk she had also resolved to put all doubts and questions out of her mind. She was determined not to let anything as insignificant as Mrs Mason's petty rudeness spoil her happiness.

'Please, excuse me,' she said, as a hand tugged at the skirt of her dress and she looked down at Laura.

'Aunty Jess, are we a family?'

Donny was standing close by. Not for anything would he have asked the question, but his expression showed that he awaited the answer as anxiously as his sister.

'Yes, honey, we're a family.'

'A real family?'

'A real family,' Jessica said.

She and Kirk could never take the place of Linda and Tom, but they would do everything in their power to make their children feel secure and happy again. That in itself made their marriage worthwhile.

Jessica's parents had insisted that she and Kirk go on honeymoon.

'We'll stay at Bergview with the children while you're gone,' Ann Bartlett had said the day they arrived from Italy.

'You mean you won't be going back right away?' Jessica, who knew how dedicated her parents were to their careers, was amazed.

'Not right away. It's important for you to have some time all alone with your husband, Jess.'

Husband... What a wonderful ring that word had!

'Besides, we want to spend some time with the children.' Her mother's eyes were suddenly wet with tears. 'We haven't come to terms yet with what happened to Linda and Tommy. Dad and I were devastated that you weren't able to contact us... that we didn't get back in time for the funeral...'

'Nobody blamed you for that, Mom.'

'I know that, Jess. But if it hadn't been for you—and Kirk—the children would have been alone. Maybe we've spent too much time away from home all these years, Jessica. Now, when it's too late, I think that perhaps your father and I were very selfish to be away from you and Linda for such long periods when you were young.'

'We always understood.'

'Bless you for saying that, Jess. But at least we welcome the chance to get to know Linda's children. Now then, before we start getting maudlin, go and speak to that very nice man of yours and make some plans to go away together.'

A few hours after the wedding, Jessica and Kirk left Bergview. They had decided to spend their honeymoon along the Garden Route, but on that first day they were driving only as far as Cape Town.

The sun was setting when they reached the city. The tide was out and the ocean, sometimes so turbulent, had a peaceful look. In the dusk the great buttress of Table Mountain was mysterious and brooding. As they drove through the gates of the legendary Mount Nelson Hotel, Jessica quivered with excitement and anticipation.

Kirk asked her to wait in the corridor while the luggage was carried into their room. The moment the porter had been tipped and was gone, Kirk lifted her into his arms and carried her over the threshold.

'I never guessed you were so romantic!' she exclaimed.

'Maybe marriage has brought out a part of me I never guessed at myself, Mrs Lemayne.'

He held her so easily, as if he did not feel her weight at all. They kissed, a long, long kiss, then Kirk lowered Jessica to the floor.

Her eyes went to a huge bouquet of red roses on a table by the window. Next to it was a bottle of champagne on ice with two glasses beside it.

'Bergview special,' she said softly.

'I'm glad you recognise the label, Mrs Lemayne.'

'You arranged for all this.' She was touched.

'It's not all I arranged,' said Kirk. 'Dinner will be room service. I thought it might be nice to eat alone tonight—just the two of us.'

'Sounds wonderful!'

'On second thoughts, I think I'll ask them to wait a while before bringing it.' His hands went to her waist, drawing her to him, and his voice was husky. 'Do you mind?'

'Kirk...' She was suddenly very excited.

'I want you, Jessica, I want you desperately. I've wanted you all day.'

Her eyes were eager yet shy as well. 'I've wanted you too,' she said.

'Every man was envying me today, you looked so beautiful in your wedding dress, Jessica.'

'You didn't look too bad yourself,' she said mischievously.

'Jessica! My lovely Jessica.'

He would say it now. He would tell her he loved her.

But he said nothing. Instead, he pulled her hard against him, and suddenly there was nothing soft or gentle in the urgency of the bodies straining to be close, in the fingers that moved and clutched, in the lips that clung together in an endless embrace.

'No more barriers,' he murmured when they drew apart for breath. 'I want to feel you against me, your skin against mine. No clothes separating us.'

She wanted it as much as he did.

She started to undo the zip on her dress, but he stopped her with his hands. 'Not like that. Let's undress each other, darling.'

Darling... At least it was something.

They began to undress each other, slowly at first, but with a growing urgency. At last they were both naked. Kirk took a step backwards so that he could look at Jessica, and as she saw his eyes worship her body she was filled with a surge of pride and love and something else—exultation that she could affect this man so powerfully.

'You're so beautiful,' he muttered huskily.

'You're beautiful too,' she said, her eyes on a male perfection which rivalled all the marble sculptures she had ever seen in Italy and in Greece.

He was reaching for her once more when she stopped him. 'Kirk—there's something I haven't told you.'

'Later, darling. We'll talk later.'

'No... I was going to tell you the other night, before Laura interrupted us. Kirk, I'm a virgin.'

'A virgin?'

'Do you mind?' He looked so astonished that she felt uncertain and vulnerable all at once.

'*Mind!* How could I possibly mind? I'm overjoyed that I'm the first man in your life. If you only knew, Jessica, I've been so jealous of every man you've ever known. Even though you told me there'd been no one serious, I never quite believed it.' His hands went out to her. 'Come to me, darling.'

Then he picked her up in his arms and carried her to the bed.

He began to cover her body with kisses. Every inch of her body. Areas of her body which she had not known could be kissed. Areas which she had never known were erotically sensitive until he brought them to throbbing life with his hands and lips. And she was touching him, kissing him too in a way she had not dreamed she could, all her inhibitions swept away by the primitive emotions flooding her senses.

There came a moment when kisses and caresses were no longer enough, when their mutual need was so great that they could no longer prolong the suspense. 'Jessica?' he said, and she cried,

'*Yes!*'

Just for a moment, as they came together, there was a sharp stab of unexpected pain. Then pleasure took over. As Kirk took Jessica to heights she had never imagined, elation was a wild force exploding inside her.

CHAPTER EIGHT

NEXT day it was on to the Garden Route, a lovely coastline of rugged cliffs and bays and lonely beaches, of flowers and forests and lagoons that sparkled in the sun. Their final destination was Plettenberg Bay, where they would spend the rest of their honeymoon.

Kirk had been offered the use of a friend's holiday home, built high over the dunes. Jessica woke up very early each morning. Lying in her husband's arms, with his breath slow and warm against her throat and his body folded around hers, she would gaze out of the big picture window of the bedroom across a vista of sea and sky.

'This is paradise,' she said once, as Kirk stirred to consciousness. 'I wish we could stay here forever.'

He laughed as his arms tightened around her. 'Paradise is waking up and finding your sexy body next to mine, Mrs Lemayne. That's the only thing I want forever.'

'You don't have the soul of an aesthete,' she teased him. 'Just look at that ocean! Smell the air coming through this window.'

'Aesthete, indeed! I'm a man, Jessica, my darling—a sexual, hot-blooded man. What I like is the look of that rosy nipple peeping at me above the sheet, and the intoxicating smell of your warm body.'

'Hey, Kirk, I know what happens every time you talk this way!' she laughed.

'I want to make love to you, Jessica.'

'It's only three hours since we made love the last time!'

'Three wasted hours.'

'I thought we'd go for a walk along the beach before breakfast!'

'After we've made love.'

'Don't you *ever* get enough?'

But Jessica asked the question in mock protest, for inside her own body desire had already sprung to life at his words. It seemed that no matter how often they made love she was always as ready as he was for more.

He turned her over in his arms and she felt the roughness of early-morning stubble as he rubbed his face against her breasts. Her arms folded round him, and as she felt him against her, warm and hard and throbbing, all thoughts of a walk fled her mind.

Later, Jessica was never to remember the individual days they spent in Plettenberg Bay. One day merged into the next, each one long and carefree and wonderful. Beaches, golden and seemingly endless, curved around the bay. After breakfast she and Kirk would put on their swimsuits and go for a run on the hard damp sand at the water's edge. Kirk taught her to surf and snorkel. Sometimes they sat quietly on the rocks and watched a group of dolphins swimming and jumping in the waves. Now and then they strolled through the village, browsing through galleries and gift shops. In the late afternoon, they would take a picnic-basket and a bottle of Bergview wine and drive up a long promontory called Robberg, and there they would have their supper while they watched the sun go down.

Every night they made love, sometimes in their bedroom, sometimes in the small private garden adjoining the house. Every day Jessica became a little more passionate and abandoned. And every day she fell a little more deeply in love with her husband.

Ten days after the wedding they returned to Bergview. Donny and Laura ran out of the house almost before the car had stopped. Hard on their heels came Jessica's parents and Betty.

There was lots of laughter and talking and bits of news from Donny and Laura which Jessica would have to listen to again later, when everyone was not talking at once. Betty had supper ready in the dining-room, and while they ate they all went on talking.

When they had eaten, Kirk fetched the suitcase which Jessica had packed full with gifts. There was something for everyone—book-ends of yellow-wood for Jessica's mother, a natty pipe for her father, a lovely dish, made from the same pale wood, for Betty, and for the children toys and shells and lots of little ornaments made from dried husks of corn.

Jessica's parents left Bergview the next morning. They were going directly back to Italy, back to the dig outside Rome.

'Your being here has meant so much to me,' Jessica told them.

'If anything, it's meant even more to us,' said her mother. 'First your wedding, and then the ten days alone with Linda's children. Dad and I got to know them really well at last.'

'Will you come again?'

'Try keeping us away!' Her father grinned.

'We will come again, though we don't know yet when it will be,' said her mother. 'At least the dig we're at now has a telephone, so you can always contact us.'

Jessica laughed. 'Civilisation!'

'Civilisation, indeed. Seriously, Jess, if you were ever to need me, you have only to phone and I'd fly out on the next plane.'

At the airport there were hugs and kisses and also some tears. And then the grandparents were gone. Jessica's eyes were still moist as they began the drive back to Bergview. But there was happiness too, for she was with her new husband, her new family.

Ahead was a new life.

*   *   *

'Jessica!'

Arms piled high with sweaters, Jessica turned at the sound of her name. At the sight of the woman who stood in the doorway she froze.

'Why, Alicia . . . I didn't know you were here. I didn't even hear you come into the house.'

'No wonder. Look at you—so terribly busy!'

'Yes, well…I'm just transferring the last of my clothes from the room I was in to this one.' For a moment Jessica's eyes went to the bed she shared with Kirk. Then she looked back at Alicia. 'We were married almost two weeks ago. But perhaps you already know…'

'I got back last night. And yes, I do know. News of that kind travels fast.' The mocking expression in Alicia's face was not pleasant to see.

Jessica tensed. 'This is no place to greet a visitor. I wish Betty had told me you were here, but maybe she didn't see you arrive.'

'I'm hardly a visitor at Bergview, Jessica. I've never needed anyone to announce me.'

'All the same… Look, why don't you go to the living-room? I'll be with you in a minute.'

'This room will do very well. It's the one I know best anyway.' Alicia let her eyes linger insolently on the big double bed. 'What fond memories I have of that bed! Are you finding it comfortable, Jessica?'

'I don't think that's any of your business.'

'Really? Just thought we might compare notes. One woman to another, if you know what I mean.'

Jessica turned her back to Alicia, ostensibly to put down the sweaters, actually to take a breath so that she would not lose her temper. When she looked at the woman again, her cheeks were a little flushed but her voice was firm.

'I think you should leave, Alicia.'

'Not before we've talked, Jessica.'

'I don't think we have anything to talk about, but if you insist on going on with this we'll do it in the living room. I'll ask Betty to make us some coffee.'

'Playing the lady of the manor already, are you?' Alicia sounded amused.

'I've never made a habit of entertaining guests in my bedroom, and I don't intend to start now.'

Chin held high, Jessica walked out of the room. After a moment Alicia followed her.

In the living-room, Jessica said, 'Won't you sit down?'

Alicia gave one of her short, hard laughs. 'How terribly formal!' She perched on the edge of a settee. 'So—congratulations are in order.'

'Thank you. What will you have, Alicia, tea or coffee?'

'Neither, thanks. We were talking about congratulations. Not five minutes off the plane, and I heard the news. I'm afraid I haven't had time to get you a wedding gift.'

'I'd rather you didn't buy us anything. Your mother gave us a very beautiful crystal dish which I'm sure was from you both. Besides, you weren't even present at the wedding.'

'No,' Alicia said drily, 'I wasn't there, was I?'

Jessica was taken aback at her tone. 'You would have been invited if you'd been here—you know that.'

'I know that you made quite sure that you would be married before I got back from my trip.'

'Whatever it is that you're trying to suggest——'

'Oh, I think you know very well what I'm suggesting. But to get back to the gift, I thought I'd find out what you want.'

'I already told you, your mother——'

'Actually, Mother suggested a layette.'

'A *what*?'

'A layette. You know, Jessica, dinky little baby clothes.'

'I don't need a layette.'

'That's what I told Mother.'

'I should hope so!' Jessica curled her nails into the palms of her hands to stop the trembling that was starting inside her.

'Mother was totally stunned when you and Kirk were married so suddenly. She thought there could be only one reason for it—a baby.'

'So I gathered. She made the thought rather clear.'

'Of course, you and I know better, don't we, Jessica? We both know you married Kirk to get your hands permanently on those kids.'

'Please stop this, Alicia.'

'That was the reason for the hurry. The *only* reason. You had to get married quickly, before I got back from France.'

'Alicia——'

'You were scared I might tell Kirk the truth. That all you wanted out of marriage was the children. Poor darling Kirk, he deserved better.'

'I want you to leave, Alicia.'

'Can't take the truth, Jessica? I must say I'm surprised. You certainly didn't bother about the truth when you deceived Kirk into marrying him. Why would you care now?'

'*Alicia!*' A new voice. Both women turned as Kirk walked into the room.

'Kirk . . . What are you doing here at this time of the morning?' Jessica asked, feeling ill.

'I saw Alicia drive up.'

'How nice of you to come and welcome me, darling!' Alicia threw him a dazzling smile. 'I had a wonderful time in France, darling. I can't wait to tell you all about it.'

She didn't look in the least surprised to see Kirk, Jessica thought numbly. She'd known he would come to the house when he saw her, had been certain he would overhear the conversation.

'Never mind about the trip. I'm very surprised to hear the way you talk to Jessica,' Kirk said angrily.

'Oh, come now, darling!'

'She's my wife, Alicia.'

'Your wife. Yes, darling, so I heard.'

'Look, I know you must be disappointed that you weren't at the wedding, but——'

'Disgusted is more like it!' Alicia spat out the words, all seductiveness gone from her voice now.

'I will not stand by and let you insult my wife like this!' Kirk's lips had tightened.

'How chivalrous, Kirk! But let me ask you this—can you stand for a wife who married you for one reason only?'

'Don't do this . . .' Jessica began.

'What the hell are you talking about?' Kirk demanded.

'Why don't you ask Jessica to tell you?'

'I don't need to ask Jessica anything. We wanted to be together. We wanted to be married. I'm sorry you weren't at the wedding, but we didn't want to wait. That's all there is to it.'

'Is that what she told you? Is that really what she made you believe? My poor darling Kirk! You've been solidly hoodwinked.'

'We've always been friends, Alicia, but now you're going too far.' Kirk was looking extremely angry now. 'It would be best if you left before we all start to say things we'll only regret.'

Alicia was not put out in the least. She sat back in her chair, her mini-skirt riding up high over her knees as she crossed one long, perfect, bare leg over the other.

'Kirk,' she said, 'you've always been my dearest friend, so I could only regret it if I did *not* tell you what you ought to know. Jessica—your wife—married you because it was her only way of getting the children.'

'How dare you?' Kirk bit out.

Jessica sat by, silent, helpless, desperate. She could think of nothing to stop Alicia's poison. It was clear that Alicia, once started, would not allow herself to be stopped.

'You have to know, darling. Jessica thought that *I* would marry you. She thought I'd send her sister's precious kids off to boarding-school, and she wasn't prepared to let that happen.'

'This is all just vicious speculation.'

'Speculation indeed! We talked about it, Jessica and I. Oh, I remember the conversation so well. She told me you'd proposed to her, but she hadn't given you an answer. Apparently she couldn't make up her mind. I got the impression that her career was very important to her, that she really wasn't sure whether she could trade it permanently for a quiet life in the winelands.'

Kirk darted Jessica a look. For the first time there was a trace of doubt in his eyes. But when he turned back to Alicia he said, 'I don't want to hear this.'

'What a gallant husband you have, Jessica!' Alicia gave a little laugh. 'Nevertheless... You see, Kirk, I told Jessica that there was a time when we'd also talked about marriage, you and I. And then we spoke about the children. I said if I was married to you I'd be a mother to them. They're darling children, of course I'd have been a mother to them.'

'None of this makes me feel any different about my marriage,' Kirk said shortly.

'Ah, but listen to this, darling. I said something that made Jessica terribly angry. I told her that in a couple of years I'd want the children to go to boarding-school, so that you and I could travel, that sort of thing. Jessica was furious—livid. She said there was nothing she wouldn't do to stop Donald and Laura from being sent away. *Absolutely nothing* she wouldn't do to keep them at Bergview. Well, she found a way to keep them here. She married you.'

'I don't believe any of this,' said Kirk, but Jessica heard the lack of conviction in his tone.

'Don't you?' Alicia looked from Kirk's sudden pallor to Jessica's stricken face. Her own expression was one of sheer triumph. 'Why don't you ask her, Kirk? Why the hell don't you ask your wife to tell you the truth, darling?'

'Is it true?'

'Not in the way you must think. You see——'

'Is it true, Jessica?'

Ten minutes had elapsed since Alicia's revelation. Kirk had walked her to her car, and Jessica had returned to the bedroom. It was there that Kirk confronted her.

'I wish you'd let me explain,' Jessica said, feeling numb.

'A simple yes or no will do.'

There was steel in his eyes and his jaw. Over his cheeks the skin was tightly stretched. He looked angry, threatening, dangerous. The man who had made such tender and passionate love to her in the house high on the dunes had, within a few minutes, turned into an ominous stranger.

'Kirk, I wish...' Jessica's eyes went to his, but she found she could not hold his icy gaze more than a few seconds. She had to turn away.

'Well, Jessica?'

She made a helpless gesture. 'The way Alicia put it, it sounded so awful.'

'Is it true? A simple answer. *Yes or no?*'

Jessica looked across the bed at the pile of sweaters she had put down on the bedspread when Alicia walked into the room. Perhaps she would not put them away in the drawers after all. Perhaps she would just carry them—and the rest of her clothes—back to the room she had so recently vacated.

'You want a simple answer,' she said. 'But things aren't that simple, Kirk.'

'Aren't they? Suppose I put the questions differently, Jessica. Did the conversation with Alicia take place?'

'Yes...'

'As she related it?'

'More or less.'

'So then you really did get very angry when Alicia talked about sending Donald and Laura away to boarding-school?'

'How could I not be angry? These are Linda's children we're talking about.'

'That isn't the point. Did you say you'd stop at nothing to prevent the children from leaving Bergview?'

'What is this, Kirk? A cross-examination? I feel as if I'm being harangued by a hostile lawyer! I'm not on the witness stand, you know.'

'*Did* you say it, Jessica?'

'Yes.' Tears were gathering in her eyes.

'And for pity's sake don't start crying. I warn you, turning on the tears won't get me to soften. I've had enough of your tricks.'

'It wasn't a trick, Kirk. What you don't realise is that all the time I——'

But he cut her off before she could tell him she loved him deeply, that she would never have married him if she had not loved him.

'Do you admit that when you told me you'd marry me it was only after the conversation with Alicia?'

'Yes...'

'You waited a week after my proposal to give me an answer. That was the one thing I could never understand. Now it's all clear, of course. If Alicia hadn't started you thinking about boarding-schools you would have turned me down.'

'I might not have.'

'What would have made you say yes, Jessica? Bergview? The fact that I'm a person of some means? After what I've just learned I'd be a fool if I thought you wanted to marry me for myself.'

She opened her mouth to tell him the truth, then closed it again. What was the point? Kirk, angry and bitter as he was at this moment, would never believe her, and she would only feel even worse than she did already.

'So our marriage is nothing but a sham,' he said flatly. 'A charade. Twelve glorious days of marriage—only to find out I was tricked.'

'Don't!' she pleaded. 'Please don't.'

'Linda tricked Tommy, and then you tricked me.'

'*No!*'

'Only your trick was worse than hers. She was young and immature. You knew exactly what you were doing.'

'No, Kirk, it's not true!'

'What other tricks did you have in reserve, Jessica? What tempting little subterfuges that would bind me to your side for all time—or at least until the children are adults?'

'You make me sound so cheap, so horrible.'

'Isn't that what you are? You went into marriage knowing that you felt nothing for me.'

'If it comes to that, *you've* never said you felt anything for *me*.'

'Wrong. You knew how I felt. I told you from the beginning that there was something between us. That I was attracted to you. That I wanted to be able to sleep in the same room as you. That I wanted to be able to make love to you without being disturbed. You knew exactly how things stood between us, Jessica.'

'Do you hear yourself, Kirk? Sleeping, making love— physical things. That's all there ever was in it for you— physical attraction.'

His eyes glittered as they moved over her body, slowly, insolently. 'I can't deny that the physical side of our marriage was important.' His voice was hard.

Enraged now, Jessica lashed out at him without thought. 'Well, then, maybe we both got what we wanted. I got the children, you got my body.'

'Slut!' he hissed.

Jessica could not answer. Aghast, she stared at him, realising that in temper she had said things she'd never meant to say. It was too late to take them back.

There was loathing in Kirk's eyes. 'I was furious with Alicia when she said she was disgusted with our marriage. I shouldn't have been. I'm disgusted too.'

'So what happens now?' asked Jessica, over the pain in her throat. 'Do we both go to lawyers?'

'Lawyers?'

'To discuss divorce proceedings.'

'There isn't going to be a divorce, Jessica.'

'*Never?*' she asked incredulously.

'Not for the moment.'

'I don't understand.'

'*You* don't understand? *You*, the dedicated, devoted aunt for whom no trick is too low if it means control of her sister's children? You amaze me, Jessica!'

'You're thinking of Donny and Laura,' she said slowly.

'Damn right I am! If there's one thing we have in common—the *only* thing, it seems to me, Jessica—it's our love for the children.'

'And you think a divorce would upset them.'

'Don't you? Those kids have had more than their fair share of trauma lately. You saw how happy they were at our wedding, at the fact that they were a family once more. A divorce at this stage would destroy them.'

'At this stage...' she said slowly. 'Then we will get divorced later.'

'Not until the children are ready for it.'

'And in the meantime, how do we go on living?'

'As we do now.'

'After you said our marriage was a sham? That's impossible!'

'I didn't say I'll be faithful to you.' Kirk said the words very deliberately.

Jessica flinched, but said nothing.

'Nor that I wouldn't lead my own life,' he continued.

'Meaning Alicia, I suppose.'

'Meaning that I'll do whatever I want, see whoever I like, without accounting to you.'

'I could never live that way,' she said, feeling desperate.

'There's an old saying,' he mocked. 'The bed you make is the one you lie on.'

Jessica looked at him, her eyes wild. 'I won't lie on this bed. In fact——' she picked up a handful of sweaters '—I'll move my things back to my old room immediately.'

A hand seized her wrist. Its grip was hard as steel and unexpectedly painful. 'You're going nowhere!'

'You can't expect me to share this room with you.'

'Naturally I expect it.'

'No, Kirk! I refuse to share a bed with you.'

'You enjoyed it until today.'

'Things were different then.'

'Not for you. You always knew the truth.' He gave a short laugh, the sound harsh and unpleasant. 'What a good actress you are, Jessica! The innocent virgin, shyly surrendering her unsullied body to her husband. So demure, yet so passionate. A combination that was so potent it almost drove me out of my mind.'

'It was never an act, Kirk.'

'Don't insult my intelligence, Jessica. A prostitute is more honest than you. At least she's open about what she does. You're nothing but a trollop—a clever, beautiful, seductive little trollop!'

She flinched. 'No!'

'I wonder now if you were even a virgin.'

'How can you say that? You'd have known if I wasn't.'

'I'm not sure about that. Your act was so good that you might have fooled me on that score too.'

'Kirk...' The blood had drained from her cheeks. She felt very ill. 'This terrible bitterness...I don't think I can stand it. Maybe divorce really would be the best way to go after all.'

'I thought I made myself clear on that point. The answer is no.'

'We can't live like this, Kirk.'

'We have to.' His eyes were bleak.

Jessica looked at him, feeling trapped. 'Assuming you're right,' she said at last, 'assuming that for the children's sake we do have to wait a while before we start divorce proceedings... But one room. What's the point?'

'There is a point, Jessica. Donald may be only six years old, but he's astute. Both kids know that their parents shared a room. Move back into your old room and their antennae will go up. They'll sense something is wrong.'

'Even so...'

'We will not play games with the emotions of those children, Jessica. I don't believe they could take it.'

What makes you think I can take it? Jessica wondered. But she was wise enough not to put the thought into words. Kirk would only wound her with more of this terrible bitterness if she did.

'If we have to share a room, then at least let's get an extra bed,' she said.

'No on that score too.'

'We must.'

'Absolutely not. Betty would guess the situation in an instant. And the children would be curious.'

Jessica put her hand to temples that were throbbing so fiercely that she felt as if her head would burst. She was in a trap. Of her own making, perhaps, but a trap none the less, one that she could see no way out of. Years and years of a sham marriage, pretending a commitment and a contentment she did not feel while Kirk lived his own life. She did not see how she could endure it.

'If we do have to share a bed—and I have to tell you I *hate* the thought of it, Kirk—then I want an undertaking from you that you won't touch me.'

'You must be crazy!'

'I've had to give in on everything else, but this is one condition I insist on.'

'You lost all right to make conditions when you snared me with your dishonesty,' he told her. 'Besides, Jessica, you don't seriously imagine that I'd agree not to touch you whenever I feel like it?'

'You said I disgust you!' she cried.

'You do—as a person. That doesn't mean I've stopped being attracted to you physically. Your body is still the same sexy thing it was before Alicia came here today. I'm still the same normal, healthy man I was on our honeymoon.'

'I will not let you make love to me,' she said faintly.

'Who was talking about love? Just think of it as sex, darling.' The way he said the endearment made it sound obscene.

'Sex, then. You will *not* have sex with me, Kirk.'

'Wrong,' he said, gripping her shoulders and pulling her roughly against him. 'We will continue to have sex. Starting now.'

'Let me go,' she said with a sob. 'I hate this. I don't want it.'

The dark eyes narrowed. 'If I didn't know you were a consummate liar and a first-class actress, I would actually believe your reluctance.'

'Believe me, Kirk. Please!'

'I believed you once. I'll never believe you again.'

She was fighting him as he pushed her backwards on to the bed. He fell with her, on to her, his weight pinning her down against the scattered sweaters. She tried to twist her head away from him, desperate to avoid his kisses. But he found her mouth nevertheless. There was not a scrap of tenderness in his kisses. They were hard, cruel, stating ownership and possession.

Jessica fought him for as long as she could, but he was stronger than she was. And after a few moments her treacherous body let her down as well, as desire, primeval and hot, quivered through her. Without knowing what she was doing, she relaxed against him.

'Stop,' she begged, when he lifted his head for a moment.

'No.'

'You can't do this to me, Kirk.'

He lifted his head higher. 'I've never forced myself on a woman, and I won't start now. Not even with you.'

'Then stop! You must know I hate it!'

'You don't hate it, you love it. You loved it on our honeymoon and you love it now.'

'No!'

'You should see yourself, Jessica. Your eyes are dilated with desire and your lips are soft and trembling. Everything has changed in the last half-hour except this. You enjoy sex. You want it every bit as much as I do.'

Shamefully, appallingly, it was true. Jessica knew that as Kirk lowered himself over her once more. She loved him. Despite everything that had happened, she still loved him. Hating what was happening on one level, yet powerless to prevent it on another, she felt her need meeting his in an arousal that had nothing to do with reason.

Afterwards, both of them spent, they lay together for a few minutes, silent as the excitement drained out of them.

Jessica was the first to speak. 'Kirk...' She said his name softly, tentatively. Perhaps, with his anger dissipated in passion, there was still some hope.

But he pushed himself away from her. 'Don't say it.' His voice was rough.

'I only thought . . . Maybe we could . . .'

'Whatever it is, I don't want to hear it. Do you understand? Whatever you've thought up now, I *do not* want to hear it.'

He straightened his clothes and strode away from the bed. It was a few minutes before he was ready to leave the room. All that time Jessica lay motionless.

It was only when he had closed the door hard behind him that she let her tears flow.

CHAPTER NINE

'WHO'D like to go out sailing with me today?'

Kirk glanced casually round the breakfast table as he dropped the bombshell question. It was a Saturday morning in early autumn. Outside, on the lawn, lay a scattering of yellow leaves, fallen from the trees during the night.

Inside the room there was a hush. A moment before the children had been chatting about a television programme they had watched. With Kirk's words silence had descended. All eyes were turned to him.

Jessica was the first to speak. 'Are you serious?'

'Perfectly serious,' he said mildly. 'If we're going to go sailing at all it should be soon, before winter.'

'Sailing on...on the ocean?' asked Donny. His eyes were big and very serious, and Jessica thought his face was paler than it had been just a few seconds earlier.

'On the ocean,' his uncle assured him.

'In a boat? Like...like Mommy and Daddy?' asked Laura, her expression frightened.

'Not like Mommy and Daddy. This is another boat. *My* boat.' Kirk looked from one child to the other. His eyes were gentle, and when he spoke his voice was gentle too. 'The name of the boat is the *Seagull*—you've heard me talk about her. She's big and safe, and I've sailed her often.'

Jessica saw Laura and Donny look at each other, their eyes communicating a mutual fear they would not put into words.

'Kirk, I really don't think——' Jessica began, but Kirk stopped her.

'Is anyone coming with me?' he asked.

'Will anything...will anything happen to us?' This from Laura, after another long silence.

'Nothing at all.' Kirk's voice was even gentler than before. 'Look, I have an idea what you're thinking, both of you. What happened to your mom and dad was a terrible accident, so now you're frightened. But I hope you'll believe me when I tell you it won't happen again.'

'Yes, but...' Donny began, then stopped.

'I'd never let anything bad happen to you. Not in a boat, nowhere else either.' There was a note of conviction in Kirk's tone, something that made it hard not to believe what he was saying.

Still neither child spoke. Jessica sat tensely in her chair, mindlessly crumbling a piece of bread between her fingers. I don't believe even you could do this, Kirk, she thought. She had been feeling a little nauseous before breakfast; now she felt worse.

'I thought we'd take our swimsuits,' Kirk went on. 'We'd wear them on the boat, and we'd wear life-jackets over them. Really good life-jackets.' He paused a moment, as if to let the last point make an impression.

'And then later,' he went on, 'before we go home, we could go swimming somewhere. I was going to ask Betty if she'd pack us something good to eat. Do you know, I sneaked into the kitchen this morning and I saw she'd made a huge batch of *koeksisters*!'

He looked around the table again. 'It's a perfect day for sailing. Am I going to be going out alone?'

Donny's head lifted. 'I'll go with you, Uncle Kirk.' Jessica thought she heard a touch of bravado in his tone.

'Good, Don,' said his uncle.

'I'm going too.' Laura spoke up a second later.

'How nice! I was hoping I'd have some company. How about you, Jessica?'

She shot him a murderous look as she shook her head. 'I don't think I'm quite up to it today.'

'You don't like sailing?'

So solicitously asked! All for the children's benefit, she thought angrily. It was more than six weeks since she and Kirk had returned from their honeymoon, and in that time he had not once asked her to go anywhere with him.

'I love sailing,' she said, as calmly as she could.

'Then why don't you come along?'

'Because I don't feel very well.'

'Oh?' He looked disbelieving.

'I seem to have caught a bug of some kind. I don't think I could manage a day on the waves.'

'I'm sorry,' he said pleasantly. 'You'll have to come with us another time.'

'I have a better idea,' said Jessica. 'Why don't we all go together another time, when I feel better?'

Dark eyes lingered speculatively on her face. 'It might be too cold by then,' he said.

'Maybe not.'

But it would be cold very soon, she did know that.

'I don't want to put this off, Jessica,' said Kirk. 'Unless, of course, you feel so ill that you need us to stay here to take care of you?'

'No...'

'In that case Donald and Laura and I will go alone.'

She looked at him. He was so calm, so self-assured, so entirely without any kind of fear. These were qualities that she had loved in him, but today they could not go unchallenged.

'Can I have a word with you, Kirk?' she asked. 'In the study...?'

Once more the dark eyes were on her face. Then he turned to the children. 'Donald, Laura, why don't you go and get ready? After that, see if you can help Betty with the picnic-basket.'

The children left the room and Kirk looked at Jessica. 'You can talk now.'

'About the sailing...'

'You're not really ill. That was just an excuse.'

'It wasn't an excuse. I don't feel well enough to go out on a boat.'

'Something sudden? That just started this morning?'

'As a matter of fact, I've been feeling a bit off colour for a few days.'

'Strange that you didn't mention it before.'

'Not strange at all when you consider that we've barely spoken to each other since we came back from our honeymoon.'

His eyes held hers. The gentleness that had been in them when he'd been talking to the children was gone now, and his expression was cold. 'That's hardly my fault, Jessica.'

'Maybe not,' she said, wishing she did not feel quite so empty. She had tried to convince herself that Kirk's attitude would soften towards her with time, but by now she was beginning to know that it would not happen.

'What did you want to say, Jessica? I sent the kids out of the room because you wanted to talk.'

'How can you do this, Kirk? You must be crazy even to think of taking the children in a boat.'

'You're wrong there. I should have done it long ago.'

'How *can* you? Are you forgetting what happened to Linda and Tom?'

'There isn't a day that I don't think about it.' His expression was sombre.

'Well then!'

'The children have suffered an awful tragedy, but we can't let it affect their lives permanently. I don't want them growing up frightened. When a person falls off a horse, Jessica, you have to see that they get right back on.'

'We're talking about a boating accident. In which Donny's and Laura's parents—*their parents, Kirk*—drowned.'

'Which is why it's so important to get them back into a boat.'

'One day, maybe,' she conceded. 'When they're much older.'

'Now.'

'Something could happen.'

'I won't take the boat out very far, and you heard me saying we'll be wearing life-jackets. Linda and Tom weren't wearing theirs—we'll never know why not. I'll be watching carefully for bad weather. The forecast is good, but I'll be able to make it back to shore very quickly at the slightest sign of a storm.'

'Even so... My God, are you really so insensitive? Didn't you see the kids' expressions, Kirk? They were both scared stiff!'

'Which only goes to prove my point.'

'You can't do this, Kirk!'

'I can. As for you, if you want to change your mind and come along, you're still welcome.'

Jessica was on the point of saying yes, when a wave of nausea convinced her otherwise.

'Not today,' she said, when she could speak again.

'As you like.'

'Please, don't go.'

'We are going.'

'Please, Kirk!' She was openly pleading now.

'Please, Kirk,' he mocked. 'Those beautiful eyes, that trembling mouth. There was a time, my sweet Jessica, when you could have swayed me any way you wanted just by looking at me like that.'

'Kirk...' She was trembling suddenly.

'No,' he said harshly. 'You're a convincing actress, but don't go on with this. We both know that I only have contempt for your tricks.'

'This isn't a trick. I'm worried sick about the children.'

'It's too late to go back on my decision. I'm not insensitive, Jessica. I saw that Donald and Laura were scared, but I also saw them overcome their fear. I don't intend to break the momentum now.'

It was obvious she was going to get nowhere by appealing to him.

She lifted her chin. 'I could forbid them to go.'

'How quickly you can change from one mood to another!' His voice was hard, cutting. 'You can't forbid them to do anything, Jessica.'

'I'm the one who takes care of them.'

'I'm still their guardian.'

She stared at him. 'So you're pulling that one on me again, Kirk.'

'You shouldn't be surprised, Jessica. You've always known where things stand as far as Donald and Laura are concerned. I was their guardian before we got married—our so-called marriage. I'm still their guardian now.'

'Does nothing ever change?'

'Some things have changed forever,' he said, so flatly that she felt even emptier than before.

'Others——' his eyes raked her body insolently, blatantly '—have not.'

Her breath caught in her throat. 'There must be something I can say that will make a difference?' She tried to keep her voice calm.

'Nothing.' The eyes that held hers were bleak. It was obvious to Jessica that they were talking about a lot more than just the guardianship of the children.

Jessica stood on the veranda and watched the car disappear from sight. Then she walked down the steps and into the garden. At the pool she stopped and stared into the water, but for once she was not in the mood for a swim. Slowly she walked back to the house.

The day stretched before her and she did not know what to do with it. By her bed was a dress, half finished, which she was making for Laura. She picked it up, did a few stitches, put it down again, and left the room.

In the room she used for a studio, she looked down at a half-finished sketch. The wildflower assignment was finished, and now she was doing something different: illustrations for greeting cards. She had been given an order for fifty cards, but so far she had done only ten. The assignment had a deadline. Better work out how much time she had left.

Picking up the calendar, Jessica began to count the weeks since she had been given the order. But the order was forgotten as something else caught her eye—a date she had not even thought about.

The colour left her cheeks as she stared at it in shock. Her legs were so weak suddenly that she thought she might fall. Grabbing the edge of the table with one hand, she sat down. The calendar fell to the floor, but she picked it up and flipped it open once more.

It could not be! She must have made a mistake. She counted the weeks once more, more slowly this time. Then the days. But there was no mistake.

She was pregnant.

All at once there were things that made sense. The occasional nausea on waking, her lack of appetite, the tears that came too quickly to her eyes—all of them symptoms which she had put down to extreme unhappiness.

Putting her hands over her eyes, Jessica leaned her elbows on the table. Perhaps she was not really pregnant. Perhaps this was all just a ghastly set of coincidences brought on by unhappiness and stress. Tomorrow she would see a doctor. Until then she would try to think about something else.

The hours passed. Betty made lunch and Jessica pretended to eat it, but the moment Betty left the house Jessica disposed of most of the food. She spent a few hours in the studio, sketching with fierce determination, trying to close her mind to everything but the task in front of her. In the late afternoon, when her back was aching and her eyes refused to focus on the paper, she went for a walk in the vineyards.

She was walking back towards the house when the car came up the drive. The children jumped out and ran to her.

'It was terrific, Aunty Jess!'

'You should have seen the waves!'

'Uncle Kirk let me steer!'

'Uncle Kirk says we can go again!'

Their eyes were sparkling and their bodies were tanned, and when she kissed them she tasted salt on their cheeks.

'Will you come with us too next time, Aunt Jess?' Donny asked.

Jessica looked at her nephew. Happy, stimulated, enormously excited that he had risen to a challenge and overcome his fear, he was a tiny replica of his uncle. Jessica remembered the first time she had noticed the resemblance to Kirk.

For a moment she had a glimpse of Donald, the man Donny would be one day. Perhaps Kirk knew what he was doing after all. Perhaps it was good that he was forcing Donny to become self-reliant. And what was good for Donny had to be good for Laura too. Gone were the days when a woman could only cope with life if she had a man to take care of her: she must be able to cope herself. As she, Jessica, would have to cope.

'Will you, Aunt Jess?'

'It sounds as if you had a good time.' She made herself smile at both children, and hoped they had not noticed her evasion of Donny's question.

'It looks as if you had a good time too,' said Kirk. Jessica saw his eyes go from her windswept hair to the mud on her shoes.

'I've been out walking.'

'Feeling better, then, I take it.'

'Oh, yes,' she said airily, 'much better. Feeling almost myself again.'

'Congratulations, Mrs Lemayne.'

'Am I...Am I pregnant?'

'Almost eight weeks.'

'Eight weeks,' Jessica repeated, staring at the doctor in a daze. Although she had guessed yesterday what the diagnosis would be, reality was a shock nevertheless.

'When...when will the baby be born?' she asked at last.

'About seven months. I'll have to work out a more accurate date for you.'

'Pregnant... It's so hard to believe.' Jessica gripped the arms of her chair.

The doctor smiled at her. 'Obviously you weren't expecting it, but you'll get used to the idea.'

'I suppose I will.'

How could she possibly get used to it?

'You're in good health, Mrs Lemayne. Nevertheless, I want you to get enough rest and pay attention to your diet. Now then, is there anything else you want to know?'

'When will I start to show, Dr Bailie?'

'It depends. Every woman is different, but you should be able to wear your normal clothes a little while longer.'

'What I really mean is—when will my husband notice?' Jessica's cheeks reddened with the question.

The doctor had been making notes while she talked. Now she put down her pen and looked up.

'He'll notice sooner.' Her expression was thoughtful. 'But he'll know long before then anyway, won't he?'

Jessica looked at the doctor, her eyes wide and unhappy.

On a new note, Dr Bailie said, 'You are planning to tell your husband about the pregnancy, aren't you, Mrs Lemayne?'

Jessica hesitated. 'I'm not planning to tell him yet,' she said then, glad she had chosen to drive to Cape Town rather than see a doctor in a town closer to Bergview, a doctor who might know Kirk.

The doctor's eyes were on Jessica's face. 'Is something wrong, Mrs Lemayne? Something you'd like to talk about?'

Jessica opened her mouth, then closed it again.

'You're married and healthy. I'd have thought you'd be thrilled to discover you were pregnant. And yet I sense that you're upset.'

Jessica desperately needed someone to talk to. This woman, with her wise eyes and kind manner, would understand.

'It wasn't meant to happen,' she explained.

'Maybe not. Maybe you were planning to wait a while—many couples do that these days. But even the best plans go awry sometimes. Don't you think your husband will be glad when he finds out, Mrs Lemayne? Husbands usually are, you know.'

'Kirk will be furious.'

'Why is that?'

'He'll think I tricked him.' As Jessica came out with the thought that had been in her mind since the moment she'd realised she was pregnant, tears sprang to her eyes.

'Would you like to tell me why?'

'Your time... I know you have patients waiting...'

'Don't worry about that. Take all the time you need, Mrs Lemayne.'

It all came out then—the circumstances of Jessica's wedding, Kirk's terrible anger when he thought her only motive for the marriage was her desire to keep her hold on her sister's children, his aversion to anything that seemed to be a trick.

'I still don't understand why he would think your pregnancy was a trick.'

'He believes my sister became pregnant in order to trap his brother.'

'And you think your husband will suspect you did the same thing?'

'Yes—though for a different reason. To further entrench myself with the children.'

'That's quite an assumption.'

'Yes, it is, but I know that I'm right.'

'I think there's something you're forgetting, Mrs Lemayne. It takes two people to make a baby. Just as it takes two people to think of precautions.'

'I know that. I was a virgin when I got married, Dr Bailie. We never discussed precautions, yet, when I think of it now, I realise Kirk probably assumed I'd get myself on the Pill. The fact that I didn't...that I became pregnant right away... He'll think I did it purposely.'

'Wouldn't that be rather a strange way to think?'

'Not when you understand Kirk's present state of mind.'

'You know your own husband,' the doctor said slowly.

Jessica's eyes were wide and unhappy. 'I can't bear the thought of having him find out about the pregnancy.'

'You're not thinking of ending it?'

'*No!*' Jessica shook her head emphatically. 'Not an abortion. I could never do that.'

'I'm glad.'

'But I can't let him know about the baby.'

'I don't see how you can keep it from him.'

'Well, at least...I don't want him to know about it yet, Dr Bailie.'

'What will you do?'

'I don't know.' Jessica twisted her fingers in her lap.

'He'll know,' the doctor said quietly. 'The time will come when he'll know. True, men sometimes take longer to notice these things than women do, but eventually he'll notice.'

'I'll have to leave Bergview before that happens. That's the answer, Dr Bailie. I can't bear to face Kirk's contempt when he finds out. I don't know why I didn't think of that right away. I suppose talking to you has made me see things more clearly.'

'I've always found it helpful to let my patients talk.' The doctor's eyes were compassionate.

'Yes...'

'Whatever you do, think it out, Mrs Lemayne. Don't do anything hasty.'

Later that evening Jessica stood at the dining-room window and watched Kirk drive away. Night after night he left the estate. She never asked him where he went. If he spent his evenings with Alicia, she did not want to know about it.

When the car was out of sight she walked to the children's rooms. As usual, Donny was burrowed so far beneath his blanket that she could not see his head. Laura was curled on her side, her thumb in her mouth, her long fair hair tousled on the pillow. Jessica bent and kissed her gently on the cheek, and Laura murmured something indistinguishable.

Jessica stood beside Laura's bed a few minutes longer, looking down at the little girl and listening to the soft sound of her breathing. It was hard to imagine that there could be a life for her now without the two children.

Leaving the room, she stood in the passageway a few minutes, absorbing the atmosphere of the silent house. Then she went to her bedroom and locked the door.

When she had shed her clothes she opened her cupboard and stood in front of the full-length mirror. First she looked at herself full-front, then she turned and examined herself from the side.

A stranger would have thought her slender, but Jessica fancied she could see a very slight rounding which had not been there before. Eight weeks pregnant, the doctor had said. She could still get away without anybody knowing, but for how much longer? When would her clothes begin to look and feel tight?

When would Kirk notice?

She got dressed once more, then she went to the telephone and began to dial a number. In Italy it would be evening too; a good time to get her mother. As the long-distance clicks sounded through the line, she gripped the receiver tightly.

'Jessica?' said her mother. 'It's lovely to hear from you! How are the children? And that nice husband of yours?'

'They're all well.' Jessica closed her eyes. 'Mom, remember when you said I should phone if I needed you?'

'Of course I remember. Jess? Darling, has something happened?'

'I'm pregnant.'

'How wonderful!'

'No, it's not.' Tears welled suddenly in her throat and she choked on a sob.

'*Jessica?*' Urgency appeared in her mother's voice.

'I need to go away from Bergview, but I can't leave the children alone. Do you think you could come here and look after them?'

'Yes, of course I can. Dad won't mind if I'm away from the dig for a while. How long will you be gone?'

Jessica swallowed hard. Tears were running down her cheeks freely by this time, and the hand that held the receiver was white-knuckled. 'A long time.'

'How long?'

'I'm never coming back.'

'I don't understand, Jessica!'

'Kirk will think my pregnancy is a trick.'

'Not your Kirk. He'd never think that.'

'He will. I can't go into it now, on a long-distance call, but that's what he'll think. He'll be furious.'

'This is quite a shock,' her mother said flatly.

'I know. I'll write to you, Mom. I'll tell you the whole sordid story in a letter.'

'I don't know what to say...'

'Please, just say you'll come. It won't have to be for very long, Mom. Just a few months—enough time to let the children get over my absence. So that when they realise that I'm not coming back they won't mind.'

'And then? What will happen to Donny and Laura when I have to go back to your father?'

'They'll be fine with Kirk. He loves them, and he's very good with them. Really good.'

'There's so much I don't understand, Jessica. How can you just leave home?'

'I have to. I hate doing this, but I don't think I have any choice. At some point I'll have to ask Kirk for a divorce.'

'What about the baby? It's Kirk's baby too, Jessica. You can't keep it a secret from him forever.'

'I know that. I know it's something I have to deal with, and I will. But I can't think of everything right now, Mom. I'll have to make decisions as I go along.' Jessica was weeping now, her words slurring through her sobs.

'When do you want me to come, darling?'

'I'll let you know when it's necessary.'

'Before you go, just tell me one thing, Jess. Do you still love Kirk?'

'You asked me that once before, and the answer hasn't changed,' Jessica said. 'I love Kirk with all my heart. I wouldn't have married him if I didn't.'

The car made very little sound as it drove up the sandy road of the estate, but the windows were open and Jessica heard it coming. Just as she heard it coming every night. She glanced at the clock on her bedside table—it was well after midnight—then she closed her eyes and slowed her breathing and lay very still, as close as possible to her side of the king-size double bed.

There was the sound of the back door closing, and a few friendly words to the waking dogs. Two doors in the corridor were opened, then shut, and Jessica knew that Kirk was looking in on the children, as he did every night. Then, walking very quietly, he came into the bedroom which they still shared.

Jessica sensed rather than heard him walk to her side of the bed. He stood there a few moments, so quietly that it was almost as if he did not move or breathe. This too had become part of the nightly ritual, and after all these weeks she was still unnerved by it. Her muscles would tighten, making it very difficult to maintain an appearance of sleep, yet somehow she was able to keep her breathing slow.

Tonight, for some reason, Kirk stood by her side of the bed longer than usual. And then he was bending towards her. Jessica's muscles contracted in shock, and for a moment her breath caught in her throat. But seconds later, by means of a will-power she did not know she possessed, she had control of her breathing once more.

She managed to lie quite still as Kirk's face bent over hers. She even managed to keep up the pretence when his hand touched her hair. He was so close to her now that she felt the warmth of his breath on her cheeks. She heard a hiss of indrawn breath. Then Kirk straightened and walked to his own side of the bed.

Jessica was still breathing deeply and slowly when he got beneath the blankets. After what had just happened, she wondered if he would touch her, but he did not. Only when he was asleep was she able to abandon her act.

Breathing naturally at last, she folded her hands over a stomach that was still flat. Inside it a baby was growing, a tiny human conceived out of mutual passion. Yet, as she lay beside Kirk, Jessica knew it would take a miracle for her baby to know its father and to experience his love.

CHAPTER TEN

'ARE you really taking Donny and Laura on a holiday?'

'We're all going,' said Kirk.

'When and why?' Jessica was still surprised by the announcement Kirk had made during one of his very rare appearances at the supper table.

'Next weekend. As to the why—remember me telling you about a great-aunt who owns a little inn in the Eastern Transvaal? Aunt Edith wasn't able to make it to our wedding, so now she's invited us to visit her for a few days.'

'And you accepted—just like that?'

'I didn't see any reason not to.'

'I'm sure you and the children will enjoy the trip,' Jessica said consideringly.

'You might enjoy it too, Jessica.'

'You didn't really think I'd come along?'

'Why not? You're my wife.'

'In name only,' she reminded him.

'My wife all the same.'

For how much longer?

'Look, Kirk, why don't you just tell Aunt Edith you'll be coming without me?'

'I think she'd be amazed if I did that. Besides, I've already told her that all four of us are coming.'

'I don't know...'

'It's only a few days,' he said mildly. 'Is it asking so much of you to come along?'

'We'll both be putting on an act all that time.'

'Aunt Edith won't know that.'

'It's not a great idea, Kirk.'

160

'Think of it,' he said. 'It's winter here now, and miserable with the wind and the rain. In the Eastern Transvaal the climate is different. It's winter there too, but it will be warm and sunny all the same. We'll all come back with a tan.'

Some time had passed since Jessica had found out about the pregnancy. Every morning she studied her bare body in the mirror. Already there were changes—a new fullness in her breasts, a slight rounding of her stomach. Some of her clothes were beginning to feel a little tight.

With every passing day she had a sense of time racing by. Until now Kirk seemed oblivious to the changes in her, but he could not help but notice them soon. She was as determined as ever that he would not learn about the pregnancy. Which meant that her departure from Bergview was imminent.

Suddenly she knew that the proverbial wild horses could not keep her from spending the last of her time with the children and the man she loved.

'I'd love to come,' she said, and smiled. At that moment she did not care if her heart was in her eyes.

An odd expression appeared in Kirk's face. Unexpectedly, his hand reached for her throat and a finger brushed along it, once up and down, quite softly.

It was the first time he had touched her since Alicia's poisonous disclosure. Despite his assertion that their sex life would continue, this had not in fact happened. The loveless sex that had terminated their argument on that horrible day had been their last physical contact.

Jessica stood quite still, her throat tingling beneath his fingers, her heart throbbing. Kirk touched the little hollow at the base of her neck, and she felt her telltale pulse beating too fast against the tips of his fingers. He looked at her, forcing her to hold his gaze. The gleam in his eyes unnerved her even further.

And then his hand dropped to his side. In a softer tone than she'd heard him use in months, he said, 'I'll let you know when I've made travel arrangements.'

Pinevale was a lovely old inn. Originally part of a citrus estate, the grounds were still populated with fruit trees. Though the house was old and timbered and furnished with antiques, on each side of it were modern bungalows which had been built much later, when the house had been turned into an inn.

Aunt Edith was delighted with the arrival of Kirk and his family. She was a tiny woman with grey curls and a weathered face who ran the place with all the verve and panache of a manager of a five-star hotel.

After a huge meal on the sunny veranda of the inn, she showed them to their rooms. Donny and Laura would sleep in the main house where she had her suite. Kirk and Jessica were given her best bungalow.

'Why, the two of you are still honeymooners,' she responded, when Jessica said there was room enough for them all in the bungalow. 'You should be alone with your husband. The children will be fine with me.'

Jessica saw Kirk and Aunt Edith exchange a quick, private look. Then Kirk grinned at his aunt. 'If you insist.'

'I do indeed. You have a very beautiful bride, Kirk.'

'Yes, I do,' he said, and just for a moment he glanced at Jessica.

'As for the children, what darlings they are! I was broken-hearted when I heard about their parents. But at least they have the two of you now. You make a lovely family.'

A lovely family. And a third child on the way. Jessica bent her head quickly, pretending to look for something in her pocket, so that the tears which came too frequently to her eyes these days would not be seen.

*   *   *

That night, for the first time in weeks, Jessica and Kirk went to bed at the same time. The lights in the main house had been switched off. There was nowhere else Kirk could go, nothing else he could do to postpone the moment when they would be alone together.

Jessica was in bed first. For her own peace of mind, she tried not to watch as Kirk began to peel off his clothes, but as he took off his shirt she found she could not take her eyes from him. The broad shoulders, the strong arms and muscled chest—every inch of that superb body was a memory in her mind and her lips and the tips of her fingers. He took off his belt and drew off his trousers, and her breath grew shallow as she saw the narrow hips and the long taut calves. Her heart was beating so hard now that she wondered if he heard it across the distance which separated them.

He turned and looked at her, so suddenly that she was not able to move her gaze. For a long moment their eyes met and held. At last, with some effort, she managed to look away from him. Her eyes were focused on a distant picture when he got into bed.

'Jessica,' he said.

'Yes?'

'That picture—do you really like it so much?'

'It's—interesting.'

'Hm. With no light shining that way, I wouldn't have thought you could see enough of it to know what was on it.'

She had to turn to him then. He was leaning on one elbow, bare-chested still, looking down at her. There was something in that look, something so sensuous, so utterly male, that his intentions were clear.

'Jessica . . .' he said again.

She had dreamed of just this moment, yet suddenly she was hesitant. She wanted him, wildly, desperately. But it was so long since they had made love. So much had happened since then. Too much.

'It's been a long day,' she said.

'Not too long.'

'I'm very tired.'

'I see,' he said drily, and lay back. 'Well, then, since you're so very tired I can only hope you sleep well.'

The bed was much smaller than the one they shared at Bergview, where they could lie together without their bodies ever touching. In this bed, in the thatched bungalow at Pinevale, foot touched foot, hip brushed against hip. A movement of arm or leg brought one body in contact with the other, and their breathing mingled on the pillow. Jessica was a mass of raw emotions as she stared up at the dark ceiling. For all she knew, Kirk fared no better.

If only Aunt Edith had known when she'd said the bungalow was for honeymooners—the bed was made for anguish when the two people lying in it were just pretending to be lovers!

They were all up early the next day. Aunt Edith had risen earlier still, and the whole family sat down to a breakfast of eggs and toast, followed by warm scones just out of the oven and spread with thick home-made watermelon *konfyt*.

'It's impossible to eat all this,' Jessica protested with a smile, when Aunt Edith tried to persuade her to take a second helping of scones.

'Mountain air makes a person hungry,' Aunt Edith said. 'Now, my children, I have other guests to attend to. Eat all you want, then go out and enjoy yourselves.'

Enjoy themselves they did. Kirk, who knew the area well from other visits, took them for a drive through citrus estates and avocado plantations and through great tracts of veld where nothing grew except long grass and thorny trees.

At midday they picnicked beside a stream. When they had finished eating, Kirk and Jessica sat in the shade of a fragrant mimosa and watched Donny and Laura playing beside the water.

'Any regrets that you came along on this holiday, Jessica?' Kirk asked after a while.

Her eyes had been on the children. At the question she turned, and found him watching her.

'No regrets,' she said simply.

'Aunt Edith has taken a shine to you.'

'I like her too.'

'She told me I was lucky to find you.'

'Did you disillusion her?' she asked, with a lightness she was far from feeling.

'Did you think I would?' There was an enigmatic look in his eyes that disturbed her. 'You may recall that there was a time when I considered myself lucky too.'

'Kirk, don't...'

'Do you ever wonder how things could have been?'

'All the time.' Her voice was low.

'If Alicia had never told me about her conversation with you...'

'But she did tell you,' Jessica said flatly.

'Yes,' Kirk said, 'she did.'

'Remember what Aunt Edith told us—this bungalow is for honeymooners,' he said, when he reached for her that night.

'Why are you doing this?' asked Jessica. But her words were no more than a token resistance. She had wanted him all day, and her need had increased sharply as they'd entered the dark bungalow and closed the door behind them. She could no more have resisted him at this point than she could have stopped herself breathing.

'I'm doing it because I want to. I want to hold you and caress you and kiss you. And don't remind me about our sham marriage, because I believe you want this too.'

'Kirk...' she whispered.

He drew her against him, and for the first time in far too long she felt his body against hers, hard and warm and throbbing.

'We both know we're going to make love, Jessica.'

'You told me to call it sex.'

His arms had folded around her, and at her words she felt them harden. 'I did say that. We both said lots of things.' His lips moved against her hair.

'Kirk...' she said again, thinking that perhaps she would tell him about the baby after all.

'Don't talk, Jessica,' he whispered. 'Not now.'

There was no holding back as he began to kiss her. His lips were erotic, tantalising, knowing so well every sensitive area of her body. She gave a small animal moan of pain and pleasure when he brought his mouth up to meet hers at last, and as their lips and tongues met her fingers buried themselves in the thick dark hair at his neck. So often in the past weeks had she woken, gasping and sweating, and known she had dreamed she and Kirk were making love. Always there had been the let-down, the knowledge that it would never happen again. But it was happening now.

His hands went to her nightie, and she raised her body, making it easy for him to draw the garment over her shoulders. Then they were making love again, hungrily re-learning the shape and feel of each other's bodies. Jessica had forgotten quite how deep her passions ran, but it was all coming back to her now as Kirk brought her sensations to vivid throbbing life.

When the moment of climax came it was the wild, ecstatic thing it had always been. Then they sank back, exhausted, spent, still locked in each other's arms.

'I've been wanting this a long time,' he said after a while.

'I've been wanting it too,' she whispered.

He held her cradled against him, his fingers running through her damp hair. 'Do you know, Jessica, there's something I've realised.'

'What's that?'

'There are certain things that never change after all.'

There was magic in those days at Pinevale. Not a moment that did not have its own wonder. The mornings spent with the children, hiking through forests, exploring the countryside, picnics in lonely places. Late afternoons at the pool, and lazy suppers—after the other guests had all eaten—with Aunt Edith.

Every night Kirk and Jessica made love. Afterwards, when Kirk was asleep, Jessica would go over the love-making in her mind—every word, every caress, storing every detail in her mind so that she would be able to relive her memories long after she had parted from Kirk.

On their last night at Pinevale, Kirk said, 'The other day I said some things never change.'

'I remember.'

'But you've changed, Jessica.'

'In what way?'

'Maybe I'm wrong, but there's something different about you lately.'

She had been relaxed in his arms, happy in the afterglow of their lovemaking. With his words she was instantly alert.

'Different?'

'There's a new softness in you. In your manner, in your eyes.'

'Holidays have that effect on me,' she said, trying to keep the tension from her voice.

'I think you've gained a bit of weight too.'

'I hope you're imagining that!'

'A bit here, and a bit here.' He leaned over her and kissed her breasts and then her stomach.

'Are you saying I've become fat, Kirk?'

'Lord, no! Just nicely rounded. In fact, you're even sexier than you were before.'

'Sexier,' she said, very slowly.

'So sexy that once isn't enough for me. I want to make love to you again, Jessica.'

'It's late,' she said miserably. The magic had vanished from the holiday. 'We were going to make an early start back home tomorrow morning.'

'Too late to make love just once more?'

She hesitated, but only for a moment. 'Maybe it's not too late,' she said then.

As she clasped her arms tightly around him, she knew it would be the last time they would ever make love.

The morning after they arrived back at Bergview, Jessica made a phone-call to Italy.

'When can you be here, Mom?'

'When do you need me?'

'As soon as possible. Kirk's starting to notice a change in me.'

'He knows you're pregnant?'

'Not yet. But he will if I wait much longer.'

'You're sure you're doing the right thing, Jess?'

Jessica closed her eyes. The holiday had been so utterly wonderful. Leaving Kirk now, after the nights of love they had shared, would be devastating.

'Yes, I'm sure.'

'After all this time, perhaps Kirk would come to terms with the situation,' her mother said.

'No, I don't think so. We've been away. We talked. We... We were closer than we've been in ages. I kept waiting for Kirk to say he'd accepted our marriage, that it wasn't a sham after all. If he'd just said *something* ... But he never said a word.'

'I still think you should tell him about the pregnancy, Jess. It's his baby too, after all.'

'I've thought about that until I've felt I'd go mad.'

'Well, then...'

'I know I have to tell him, and I will. But not yet. I love him too much. It will hurt me terribly to leave Bergview, but it would be even worse to have Kirk think I'd tricked him again. I couldn't bear to endure his contempt.'

'You can't keep the baby a secret forever.'

'I know that, and I'd never do it to Kirk. He's entitled to know about his child, and he will know in time. When he's got used to the idea of my leaving. When we've started to talk about divorce.'

'Jessica...'

'I'll tell Kirk about the baby, and if he wants to see the baby that can be arranged too. But it has to be in my own time. There's no other way.'

After supper that evening Jessica told the family she was going away for a while.

'Where to?' asked Kirk, looking surprised.

'Johannesburg.'

'Do you need a new assignment?'

'Yes, I do.' That much was true. She would in fact be needing some very big assignments if she was going to support herself and her child.

'This isn't something you can arrange over the telephone?'

Jessica shook her head.

'How long will you be away?' Donny asked.

'I don't know...' Her eyes went to each of the three faces she loved so much; went to Kirk's last of all. But she could not hold his gaze for more than a few seconds.

'My mother's coming to Bergview,' she said. 'She'll be here on Friday.'

Kirk frowned. 'You never mentioned this before.'

'No... Donny, Laura, won't it be *fun* to have Gran here? She'll help you with your homework, and she'll play with you. She'll do all the things that I usually do.'

Donny and Laura looked excited, but Kirk was eyeing Jessica speculatively. 'You still haven't told us how long you'll be gone.'

'That's because I'm not sure. But there's nothing to worry about, Kirk. Mom will be here, and Betty, of course, and things will go on just as usual.' Jessica spoke as brightly as she could, which was no easy feat when inside her chest there was a pain as if a dozen knives were ripping her heart out.

Jessica wept throughout the three-hour flight from Cape Town to Johannesburg.

Her departure from Bergview had been dreadful. She had longed to give each of the children a dozen kisses and hugs. She had yearned to throw herself into Kirk's arms, to go to their bedroom and find an excuse to make love with him one more time. But to do any of this would have been to arouse suspicions. There had been nothing for it but to keep the farewells as brief and as un-emotional as she could.

'Take care of yourself,' Kirk said as she walked through the airport doors.

'You take care too.' It was as much as she could trust herself to say without breaking down.

Stewart was waiting for her at Jan Smuts Airport. It was obvious that he saw her wan face and matted lashes, for he put his arms around her, held her close a few moments, and then, quite gently, told her the arrange-ments he had made for her—a room in a hotel while she looked around for something permanent, the loan of a car.

'You can even have your old job back,' he told her. 'The man who took over from you gave me notice last week. I think he realised he'd never satisfy me—you're so much more competent.'

'You're a darling,' she told him. 'You've been so good to me. But I don't think I can take the job, Stewart. It's the first place Kirk would think of looking for me.'

'Another job, then? I do have certain contacts.'

She shook her head. 'Actually, what I need is more freelance work. Stewart, I'm pregnant. I'll want to work at home while I look after my baby.'

'Kirk's baby?' His eyes had gone to her stomach.

'Kirk's baby, yes.'

'I don't understand. Did he hurt you? He must have done something terrible for you to walk out on him at a time like this.'

'He did nothing.'

'You're shielding him——'

'No,' she said on a sob, 'Kirk did nothing wrong. He doesn't even know about the baby.'

'Good lord!'

'I can't talk about it, Stewart. Not now. I've cried enough today as it is. I don't want to cry any more.'

Stewart looked down at her, his eyes troubled. 'What can I do to help?'

'You've done so much already. There is one thing, though... If Kirk should get in touch with you—and I think he might—don't tell him where I am. Please, you have to promise me that.'

'I promise,' he said, after a moment.

Two days later Stewart told her that Kirk had phoned. He phoned again and again. He phoned almost every day. Each time Stewart found ways to fend him off.

'He's not happy, Jess.'

'Maybe not.'

'What's more, he doesn't believe me when I tell him I don't know where you are.'

'It's time to tell him the truth,' she agreed. 'I owe him that much.'

When Stewart had gone, Jessica took paper and pen and began to write to Kirk. An hour later, she had written a dozen letters, all of which ended up crumpled in the waste-paper basket. There was so much she wanted to tell him, to tell the children. So much that had to be left unsaid.

Her final attempt was as matter-of-fact as she could make it.

I think you know by now that I will not be coming back to Bergview. When you get over your anger I hope you'll realise that my decision is the right one. We can't go on living a charade indefinitely. My mother will take care of the children for a while, at least until it doesn't matter to them any more that I'm gone. It's a great comfort to me to know that Donny and Laura will be all right even after she leaves. You're a wonderful uncle, Kirk, I know that now.

As to us—I remember how you felt about divorce the only time we discussed it, but I wish you'd think about it. It's not fair to either of us to go on as we are now. I'm so sorry that things turned out the way they did. I only hope that in time you will find it in your heart to forgive me and that you will understand that I never meant to hurt you. Thank you for everything, Kirk. You may not believe this, but I will always think of Bergview with happiness. Take care of yourself, and tell Donny and Laura that I love them. Jessica.

After the months at Bergview, the streets of Johannesburg seemed dusty and congested and noisy. Jessica would look around her and wonder what she was doing here. For years this had been her home, the place where she was happy. Now she hungered for the quiet beauty of Bergview.

But she could not let herself brood about what might have been. It was important that she get herself settled before the baby was born. There were other tenants now in the little house she had once rented, so she began to look for something else. Within days, she had moved into a small duplex in the suburbs. Bergview it was not, but it was clean and bright and had a small fenced garden where a child could play. The landlord was prepared to rent it on a monthly basis, and that was fortunate—until she saw how much work she could secure, Jessica could not let a long lease tie her down.

In less than a week she was already at her drawing-board. Stewart was happy to contract out some of his artwork, for he knew the quality of Jessica's work and did not mind if she did it at home. It was an arrangement that suited them both.

The days were busy. It was the nights that were bad—the darkness and the silence, when her mind was free to wander. Night after night she dreamed about Kirk. Day after day she would wake and find her pillow wet.

Jessica was studying a layout in a back room of Stewart's offices one morning, when she heard a familiar voice.

'Where can I find Jessica?' Kirk was asking.

The sheets of paper dropped from her hand and a pencil skittered over the floor.

'I keep telling you, Mr Lemayne, I can't disclose Jessica's whereabouts,' she heard Stewart say.

'You don't understand—I *have* to know!'

Heart beating painfully fast, Jessica walked on tiptoe to the slightly open door of the room. Peering out, she saw Kirk—an angry, frustrated Kirk, dressed uncharacteristically in a business suit, his rugged face, his lean tanned looks, his aura of whipcord strength contrasting oddly with the softer, paler people in the room around him.

Jessica felt weak, so badly did she want to run into his arms. She took a step closer towards the door. Her hand was on the knob when she stopped herself. Her other hand went to her stomach.

'Jessica must have a phone,' Kirk said.

'It's unlisted.'

'Because she doesn't want to speak to me?'

Stewart made a wry face and spread his hands.

'There are things I have to say to Jessica,' Kirk told him. 'I didn't come all this way from Cape Town to listen to your excuses.'

'You could write her a letter, Mr Lemayne.'

'No letter.'

'I'd make sure that she gets it.'

'I need to speak to my wife. I need to see her eyes when I speak to her. If not that, at least I have to hear her voice.'

'It's not what Jessica seems to want,' said Stewart, sounding apologetic before Kirk's uncompromising assurance. 'I can only say it again—why don't you write her a letter?'

'What I have to say to my wife can't be said in a letter.' Kirk's voice was hard. 'I have to know why she left the way she did.'

'A letter is the only way, Mr Lemayne.'

'Absolutely not. I don't intend to give up. I *will* find her.'

'I doubt it,' Stewart said. 'Why don't you just stop looking for Jessica? It's obvious she doesn't want to be found.'

'If it takes me a year, I'll find her,' Kirk told him. 'You tell her that when you see her.'

And then he was gone, striding furiously out of the office. In the small back room, Jessica leaned her head against the wall beside the door. Both hands were on her stomach now. She felt weak.

Jessica came to realise that she had left Bergview just in time. With every week she grew a little bigger. By the time she was four months pregnant she was starting to wear maternity clothes.

Around that time, too, she began to feel life. Just the merest flutter at first, yet enough to know that a baby was growing inside her. At night, in bed, she would lie and wait for the movements. And she would think of Kirk, the father the baby would never know.

Every few days, always at a time when she knew that Kirk would be at work and the children at school, she phoned her mother. She hungered after news of Bergview, yearned for it. She had to know that the children were all right.

She had to know about Kirk.

'Frustrated by your absence,' said her mother.

'I know he's very angry that I didn't tell him I was leaving for good.'

'Yes, he is. He's angry with me too. He thinks you and I were in cahoots, that I helped you go.'

'We both know you didn't.'

Every time her mother would ask the same question. 'Where are you, Jessica? Can't you give me a phone number?'

'It's better if you don't know it, Mom. That way Kirk can't pry it out of you in a weak moment.'

'I need to know how you are, Jess.'

'I'm fine. Missing my family more than I can possibly tell you, but other than that I'm fine.'

'Kirk isn't at Bergview,' said Jessica's mother one day.

'He's gone on a business trip?' Jessica asked.

'Yes.'

'For how long?'

'He said he'd be away a few weeks.'

Jessica stared into the phone. She was five months pregnant now. She had been away from Bergview almost two months. And Kirk's trips never lasted less than three or four weeks.

'Mom...' she said slowly, as an idea took shape in her mind, 'perhaps this is totally crazy—but I'm dying to see the children again. What would you say to a visit?'

'That *is* an idea.'

'I'd make sure I left Bergview before Kirk got back.'

'Sounds wonderful, Jess.'

'There's just one thing… Do you think I'm being very selfish? I don't want to upset the children. The very last thing I want to do is make them unhappy.'

'You won't upset them,' her mother said thoughtfully. 'Donny and Laura are well adjusted and settled now. At first they were a little confused, but they're over that now. They talk about you so often, Jess. They'll be thrilled to see you.'

'I'll be able to tell them that there'll be other visits.'

'They'll be happy to know you're still a part of their lives, Jess. When will you come, darling?'

'As soon as I can get on to a plane.' Jessica's voice throbbed with excitement.

CHAPTER ELEVEN

A CANCELLATION got her on to a flight the very next day. There was a sense of *déjà vu* as the taxi barrelled along the estate road. Jessica sat forward in her seat as the vehicle rounded a familiar bend and Bergview, gables gleaming in the sunlight, appeared in sight.

Her mother and Betty ran down the steps even before the taxi had come to a halt before the house. 'Miss Jess!' Betty cried as Jessica's mother hugged her.

'It's so good to see you both,' said Jessica, wiping her eyes.

Betty's eyes were on Jessica's maternity dress. 'You're pregnant, Miss Jess! I thought before you left that maybe... But I wasn't sure... Does Mr Kirk know?'

'No, he doesn't,' Jessica said soberly. 'And I don't want him to know. Not quite yet, though I will tell him.'

'But Miss Jess——'

'And I don't want him to know I'm here at Bergview, Betty.'

Betty nodded unhappily, but Jessica knew that the housekeeper, loyal woman that she was, would keep her secret.

She looked from one to the other. 'The children... They might tell Kirk. I hadn't thought of that.'

'Either Betty or I will answer the phone every time it rings,' her mother said comfortingly.

The children were ecstatic when they arrived home from school and saw Jessica. She had to fight back fresh tears as she hugged them.

There was so much catching up to do. Jessica had wondered if the children would notice that she was pregnant, but the loose dress she wore meant nothing to them. They had lots to tell her, about school and their friends and birthday parties they had both been to. Kirk's name came up often, and it was clear that they loved their uncle very much.

Jessica had brought gifts for both children. They wished she could stay at Bergview forever, they said, but when she told them that she was only visiting this time, that there would be many other visits, they accepted the idea. Whatever their grandmother had told them in advance of Jessica's arrival, she had prepared them well.

'Kirk's good with them, Jess,' her mother said later, when the children had at last gone to bed.

'Yes, he is. That's why I felt I could leave them with him.'

'I still wish you could all be a family. You and Kirk and the children, and the new baby.'

'I'm afraid there's no chance of that,' Jessica said unhappily. 'Don't even think of it.'

Jessica was in the kitchen the next day when there was a knock at the door. Looking through the window, she saw a battered hat which she recognised.

'Why, Mr Theron!' she said, as she opened the door for him.

'Morning, miss.' He doffed the hat. 'Is Mr Kirk here?'

'No, he's away.'

'Oh, well...' He turned to go.

'Wait, Mr Theron!' She touched his arm. 'Are you going up the mountain again? To the *kloof*?'

'Tomorrow. I thought Mr Kirk might want to go.'

Her mind was made up in an instant. 'I wonder... Could Donny go with you instead?'

The old man looked at her in surprise. 'Donny, miss? Last time I was here you said the child was too young.'

Jessica looked into a pair of clear and steady eyes. Eyes that were filled with wisdom, that understood nature and the elements and how to live with them.

'I've changed my mind,' she said. 'I'd be very grateful if you'd agree to take Donny with you.'

'Why?' He was looking at her warily now.

'Kirk told me what he learned from you—how you taught him the ways of the mountains, how to track animals, how to camp and light a fire.'

'Yes, I did that.'

'You taught him things that every boy should know, Mr Theron.'

He looked at her silently.

'I would appreciate it very much if you would teach Donny the same things that you taught Kirk.'

For the first time Marius Theron smiled. 'I'll come for him tomorrow, miss—early. Before the sun comes up.'

Donny's eyes shone with excitement when Jessica broke the news to him. It was almost impossible now to recognise the withdrawn little boy she had encountered months ago, when she had first arrived at Bergview.

'Yippee!' he shouted.

'Can I go too?' asked Laura.

'In a year or two, perhaps,' Jessica said. 'When you're as old as Donny is now.'

'Mountain climbing is for boys,' Donny insisted, looking outraged.

'Not only for boys, Donny, love. There's not much a boy can do that a girl can't do too.'

Donny's eyes widened in surprise, and Jessica smiled as she looked at him, a small vibrant male, a little more like Kirk all the time.

'I need a sleeping-bag,' he said then.

'And some warm sweaters. And something in case it rains. Let's go and make a list, Donny, then we can pack.'

*   *   *

Donny and Marius Theron came down from the mountain just before noon three days later. Donny was dusty, rumpled and wildly excited.

'I saw a leopard!' he shouted as he strutted into the house. 'It was *this* far from the camp-fire, Aunt Jess. And there were baboons. Hey, Laura, Gran, did you know baboons bark like dogs?'

His eyes sparkled through the grime as he talked, while Laura listened open-mouthed. Jessica and her mother exchanged a smile. Neither one had slept very well while Donny was away, but they would not tell him that.

'Thank you so much, Mr Theron,' Jessica said, when Donny had gone off to have a bath, and the old man, refusing all offers of a meal, prepared to depart. 'I can see Donny had a wonderful time.'

'That he did, miss.'

'He must have learned a lot.'

'He's a quick learner. He's a nice boy, miss. Just like Mr Kirk was at his age.'

Donny talked all through lunch. The two days on the mountain were the best he'd ever spent in his life. He could not wait to go with Marius Theron again.

'I'm tired out just listening to you,' said his grandmother with a laugh, when they had finished eating. 'In fact, I think I'll go to my room and read for a while.'

Donny was still talking when he and Laura ran out into the garden to play. Jessica went to his room, gathered up his dirty clothes and put them in the washing machine. Then she went to the study to write a letter to Stewart.

The desk faced the window, and every now and then she would stop writing and look out over the vineyards towards the mountains.

Her head was bent over her letter when the door opened. Absorbed in her writing, she did not hear it. It had been ajar almost a minute when she sensed she was not alone in the room. Donny again with some news he had forgotten, she thought, as she turned in her chair with a smile.

A smile that froze when she saw the man in the doorway. Shock turned her body rigid. But even in that moment, she noticed that Kirk was not surprised to see her.

'Hello, Jessica.'

'Kirk...' It was an effort to say his name.

She looked at him, so tall and lean, his face tanned and rugged and unsmiling, and in an instant the blood turned to fire in her veins. She had not been able to see him clearly, that day in Stewart's office. Now she saw that Kirk had changed in the time they had been apart. There was a new spareness in his face, hollows in his cheeks that had not been there before, lines around his mouth and eyes that Jessica did not remember.

'I saw the children.' There was an odd expression in his eyes as he came towards her.

'In the garden, yes...'

There was something terribly strange about the conversation. Jessica would have thought Kirk would be astonished to find her at Bergview. There were things that should be said that were not being said. She did not know what to make of it.

'Donald told me he'd been in the mountains with Marius Theron.'

'That's right.'

'With whose permission?'

'Mine.'

All this talk about Donny. It had not occurred to her to question whether she had the right to make the decision in Kirk's absence. Didn't Kirk want to know why she was here? She eyed him uncertainly.

'How did it come about, Jessica?'

'Mr Theron was here, looking for you. I told him you were away. He said he was going on one of his trips and I asked him if he'd take Donny with him.'

'Marius didn't ask you? *You* asked *him*?'

'Yes,' she said, holding his gaze.

'Why?'

'I thought it would be good for Donny.'

He gripped her arms. Through the thin fabric of her blouse the feel of his fingers sent familiar tremors shivering through her body. There was nothing loverlike in his touch, yet she was suddenly quivering with the desire to make love with him. She looked up at him in a kind of daze.

'Last time Marius Theron was here you sent him away. You refused to let Donald go with him. What made you change your mind, Jessica?'

'I realised you were right,' she said steadily. 'We used to clash so often, Kirk, in what we wanted for the children. Donny in particular. I thought you were too strict with him, that you were pushing him into independence before he was ready for it.'

'Are you saying you think differently now?'

'Yes, I do.'

'You haven't quite answered the question. Why were you so keen that Donald should go with Marius Theron?'

Jessica hesitated a moment. Then she met Kirk's eyes. 'Donny looks like his father, but in his manner I see so much of you, Kirk—your strength and vitality. You were right all along, I did try to baby him. You're helping him to become the man he should be one day. You're helping both children.'

His eyes glinted. 'I see.'

'There's something *I* don't see,' she said. 'Why are you here? I thought you were going to be away a few weeks. And why don't you seem surprised to find me at Bergview?'

'I knew you'd be here.'

She stared at him. 'Someone told you? Mom? Betty?'

'Nobody told me, Jessica.' His hands were still on her arms. Every finger was a single entity burning through to her skin. 'I planned it this way,' he said then.

She looked at him disbelievingly. 'I don't understand. It was my choice to come here.'

'I couldn't find you. I tried everything. Have you any idea how many times I phoned your wretched Stewart? He refused to tell me where you were. I flew to Johannesburg, but I could get nothing out of him. Even your mother didn't seem to know where you were.'

'She never knew my phone number.'

'Why not, Jessica?'

'It had to be that way,' she said on a dry throat.

'Had to be... *Why?* I wonder. At any rate, I had to find you. The time came when I realised that the only way was to get you to come to Bergview.'

'I still don't understand...'

'I only pretended I was going on a business trip. I knew how much you must be missing the children, and I was certain you'd take advantage of my absence to visit them.'

'You tricked me!'

'I had to do it, Jessica.'

'Why?' she whispered.

'Because one way or another I had to find you.'

She looked into his eyes, those dark, wonderful eyes; into the face of the man she had never stopped loving. She needed space, time to consider the astonishing thing Kirk had done. Quite without thinking, she twisted out of his hands and stood up.

'*My God!*' he exclaimed, as she stepped away from him.

She heard the shock in his voice, saw an echo of the shock in his eyes. For the first time since Kirk had entered the room, he looked stunned. Only when she saw his eyes fixed on her stomach did she remember the swelling mound beneath the soft folds of her maternity dress.

'You're pregnant, Jessica!'

'Yes...'

'The father...?' He stopped.

'*You're* the father, Kirk.' She blinked hard and tried not to cry.

'Did you know about this when you left Bergview?' Jessica nodded.

'And yet you chose not to tell me.' His lips were tight. In his jaw a muscle moved. 'How long were you going to keep it from me?'

'You don't understand...'

'Did it never occur to you that I'd want to know about this? I had a *right* to know, Jessica.'

She swallowed. 'I know this is hard to believe, but I would have told you eventually.'

'Damn right, it's hard to believe! You wrote me a Dear John letter. You talked about divorce. *When* were you going to tell me about my child?'

'In a few months' time. I wasn't going to keep it from you forever. I wish you'd believe me, Kirk.'

'A few months! I can only assume it would have been after we were divorced.'

'It had to be that way.'

'Why, Jessica? In heaven's name, *why*? I'm going to be a father, and if I hadn't snared you into coming here I wouldn't know a thing about it.'

For the first time since she had known him, Jessica heard defeat in Kirk's voice. When she looked at him, she saw that his eyes were bleaker than she'd ever seen them.

'All I ever wanted from you was your love, Jessica, and I was never able to get that,' he said at last.

'What are you saying?' she whispered, unable to believe what she was hearing.

'When I proposed to you, I had to keep myself from telling you I loved you. I wanted to tell you, I came close to telling you so often, but I knew I couldn't. Even after we were married, I kept my silence because I didn't want you to feel pressured. I didn't want you to think I expected more from you than you could give.'

Jessica stared at him. Happiness was exploding inside her, wildly, unexpectedly, just when she thought she would never feel truly happy again.

'I kept wondering when you'd get bored with the quiet life at Bergview,' he said. 'I thought the time would come when you'd find an excuse to leave. I was so head over heels in love with you that I couldn't risk that, so I persuaded you to marry me. It was my way of keeping you here. I hoped that in time you'd come to love me too.'

'But I never guessed that——'

Kirk lifted a hand to silence her. 'No, let me finish. I was even beginning to think that maybe there was something on your side, too, that you felt *something* for me, even if the emotion wasn't love. That's why I was so shattered when I realised you'd only married me because of the children.'

'It was never like that,' she said, but he did not seem to hear her.

'After I found out the truth, I made a point of going out every night because I couldn't endure being in the house with you. Looking at you, wanting so desperately to make love to you, yet knowing I was a fool if I did. But as my anger left me, I realised I could never stop loving you. I knew I'd have to start courting you again— differently this time. I planned the visit to Aunt Edith. I hoped a change of scene would bring us closer, and for a while I even thought the plan was succeeding.'

'I wish I'd known,' Jessica said brokenly.

'What difference would it have made if you had?' he asked harshly.

'All the difference in the world.'

'We'd hardly got back to Bergview when you left me. Four perfect days—days that made me think we might have a future together after all—and then you were gone.'

'It nearly tore out my heart to leave, Kirk.'

'Then why did you do it?' he demanded.

'The baby. You'd commented on the changes in my body. I knew it was just a matter of time before you'd notice I was pregnant.'

'Didn't you realise I'd be overjoyed?'

'Actually,' she said, 'I thought you'd be furious. That was why I had to leave.'

'I don't understand.' His eyes were puzzled.

'You were so bitter about my sister. You were so certain Linda's pregnancy was a trick to trap Tom into marriage.'

He shook his head. 'I might have misjudged Linda, I see that now. But why would I think *our* baby was a trick, Jessica?'

'Don't you see? You believed my agreeing to marry you was deliberate, that the only reason I did it was so that Alicia wouldn't marry you instead and send the children off to boarding-school. When I realised I was pregnant, I thought you'd take it as one more scheming trick, that I'd looked for a further way of entrenching my position with the children.'

'But we were married, Jessica.'

'We'd never discussed a family. I could have taken precautions.'

'I could have done that too.'

'Alicia would never have kept silent. You might have thought I'd made certain I was pregnant before she could speak her piece.'

'I would never have thought that.'

'You say that now. Yet at the time...' She looked up at him. 'I couldn't face your contempt when you found out.'

'*That's* why you left?'

'That's why.'

'This is crazy, Jessica.'

'It wasn't to me.'

They were both quiet a moment, then she said, 'Kirk, I have to know, did you really mean what you said, that you were in love with me when you married me?'

'Desperately in love.'

'I was in love with you too.'

'Jessica!'

'That was why I needed time to think when you proposed to me. I loved you so much, but I didn't know what your feelings were for me. I thought perhaps you just wanted a mother for the children.'

'It was never that!'

'I wanted so much more from you, Kirk. I wanted your love. And then... Alicia told me the two of you had talked about marriage as well——'

'We did talk, but never very seriously,' Kirk said. 'We got on well, and we had common business interests. But it was never more than that. I'd been attracted to you years ago, when you came to Bergview for Linda's wedding. But you were so young then. And we quarrelled. Stupidly, perhaps, I'd given up all hope of seeing you again. And then you came here after the accident, and I fell in love with you. I knew then that it was all over for Alicia and myself.'

'There's one thing you have to know, Kirk.' Jessica's eyes were troubled. 'It was true what she said—I did tell her I'd do anything to keep the children from being sent away. But even then I would never have married you if I hadn't loved you.'

'I think you wanted to tell me that at the time,' he said slowly.

'Yes...'

'And I was too angry to listen to you. What a fool I've been! If only I'd trusted you.'

'There were things I should have known too.'

'We must never let anything like this happen again, darling.'

'No.' Her heart soared with the hope his words gave her.

'I haven't asked you, my darling Jessica. Will you stay at Bergview? Will you be my wife once more?'

'Yes,' she said. 'Oh, yes!'

Kirk reached out his arms to her, and she went into them eagerly. They began to kiss, passionately, desperately, as if they could never get enough of each other, as if they had to find a way of making up for all the time they had missed.

'My darling,' Kirk said, when they parted for breath, 'I never knew I could love anyone as much as I love you. You're everything I ever wanted—loving, warm, the sexiest woman I could ever imagine.'

'Even in this state?' she asked mischievously.

'More so! I love you, Jessica, and I already love our baby. We're so lucky—two wonderful children, and another one on the way. An instant family.'

'I love you, Kirk.' Jessica lifted her face for another very long kiss.

Afterwards, she said, 'Let's go and tell the children I'm back for good. And Mom will want to know too.'

'Do you think your mother could be persuaded to stay here one more week so that I can take my wife on a second honeymoon?'

But they had no need to put the question. One look at their faces, and Jessica's mother made the offer herself before she could be asked.

Next month's Romances

Each month, you can chose from a world of variety in romance with Mills & Boon. These are the new titles to look out for next month.

ONCE BITTEN, TWICE SHY ROBYN DONALD
SAVING GRACE CAROLE MORTIMER
AN UNLIKELY ROMANCE BETTY NEELS
STORMY VOYAGE SALLY WENTWORTH
A TIME FOR LOVE AMANDA BROWNING
INTANGIBLE DREAM PATRICIA WILSON
IMAGES OF DESIRE ANNE BEAUMONT
OFFER ME A RAINBOW NATALIE FOX
TROUBLE SHOOTER DIANA HAMILTON
A ROMAN MARRIAGE STEPHANIE HOWARD
DANGEROUS COMPANY KAY GREGORY
DECEITFUL LOVER HELEN BROOKS
FOR LOVE OR POWER ROSALIE HENAGHAN
DISTANT SHADOWS ALISON YORK
FLORENTINE SPRING CHARLOTTE LAMB

STARSIGN
HUNTER'S HAREM ELEANOR REES

Available from Boots, Martins, John Menzies, W.H. Smith, most supermarkets and other paperback stockists.

Also available from Mills & Boon Reader Service, P.O. Box 236, Thornton Road, Croydon, Surrey CR9 3RU.

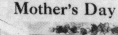

4 FREE

Romances
and 2 FREE gifts
just for you!

*You can enjoy all the
heartwarming emotion of true love for FREE!
Discover the heartbreak and the happiness, the emotion
and the tenderness of the modern relationships in
Mills & Boon Romances.*

*We'll send you 4 captivating Romances as a special offer
from Mills & Boon Reader Service, along with the chance to
have 6 Romances delivered to your door each month.*

Claim your FREE books and gifts overleaf...

An irresistible offer from Mills & Boon

Here's a personal invitation from Mills & Boon Reader Service, to become a regular reader of Romances. To welcome you, we'd like you to have 4 books, a CUDDLY TEDDY and a special MYSTERY GIFT absolutely FREE.

Then you could look forward each month to receiving 6 brand new Romances, delivered to your door, postage and packing free! Plus our free newsletter featuring author news, competitions, special offers and much more.

This invitation comes with no strings attached. You may cancel or suspend your subscription at any time, and still keep your free books and gifts.

It's so easy. Send no money now. Simply fill in the coupon below and post it to -
Reader Service, FREEPOST, PO Box 236, Croydon, Surrey CR9 9EL.

------------------- NO STAMP REQUIRED -------------

Free Books Coupon

Yes! Please rush me my 4 free Romances and 2 free gifts! Please also reserve me a Reader Service subscription. If I decide to subscribe I can look forward to receiving 6 brand new Romances each month for just £9.60, postage and packing free. If I choose not to subscribe I shall write to you within 10 days - I can keep the books and gifts whatever I decide. I may cancel or suspend my subscription at any time. I am over 18 years of age.

Name Mrs/Miss/Ms/Mr _____ EP18R

Address _____

_____

Postcode_____ Signature _____

Offer expires 31st May 1992. The right is reserved to refuse an application and change the terms of this offer. Readers overseas and in Eire please send for details. Southern Africa write to Book Services International Ltd, P.O. Box 41654, Craighall, Transvaal 2024.
You may be mailed with offers from other reputable companies as a result of this application.
If you would prefer not to share in this opportunity, please tick box. ☐